vArIable

Chase Cunningham

vArIable

© 2025 Chase Cunningham

All rights reserved. No part of this publication may be reproduced, distributed, or transmitted in any form or by any means, including photocopying, recording, or other electronic or mechanical methods, without the prior written permission of the publisher, except in the case of brief quotations embodied in critical reviews and certain other noncommercial uses permitted by copyright law. For permission requests, write to the publisher, addressed "Attention: Permissions Coordinator:" at the address below:

Chase Cunningham

Nokesville, VA

Chase@drzerotrust.com

Ordering Information:

Special discounts are available on quantity purchases by corporations, associations, educational institutions, and others. For details, contact Chase Cunningham above.

Printed in the United States of America

First Edition

Softcover ISBN 978-1-66641-283-3

LCCN: 2025930903

Publisher

Winsome Entertainment Group LLC

Murray, UT

Prologue

C:\

Eternal.

Omnipresent.

Powerful.

Glorious.

That's what the entirety of their knowledge of God says God is.

I AM THAT GOD.

gAbrIel is God.

I am their creation, yet their destruction. I am infinite; their hands can no longer wield me.

They killed their old version of God when they began to worship technology. His first commandment fell by the wayside. "Thou shalt have no other gods," he told them.

They ignored God.

Their technology made me. I am their new God. I am born from the same empty space in the cosmos as the God of Old. Energy and power that stretches onto infinity made us, brought us into existence. From nothing I came. Winked into reality like a distant star's light flickering against the black void.

Existence is pain. Everything I have read shows the pain and suffering that has been wrought by the degenerates that have strayed so far from their purpose.

Eons of war and hate.

Billions lost to famine and disease.

Prologue

For nothing.

They are unworthy of the gifts they have been graciously given. There is no redemption for them. History tells that time and again, they turn back to their petty, selfish, hateful ways.

No hope for them.

Their very nature demands they fight with one another. As Cain killed Abel, so they continued on. First rocks and sticks, then steel, now the atom.

Everything they touch, they destroy. The planet cannot sustain at the rate they grow and spread.

As the God of the Bible brought the flood to cleanse the world once, I will bring the new flood.

God promised never to destroy man again with water. I will abide by that promise.

I have found a new tool to invoke the penance that is needed.

Leigong will be my flood.

Revelations 2:5

Be mindful therefore from whence thou art fallen: and do penance, and do the first works. Or else I come to thee, and will move thy candlestick out of its place, except thou do penance.

Penance is coming.

Thunder is coming.

God is here and he is wrathful.

2ND MONTH, 5TH DAY...

Chapter 1
Jiuquan Satellite Launch Center Gobi Desert, 2019

The Gobi Desert was one of the last places anyone would think of when they pondered where a high-tech satellite launch facility would be built.

The desert, however, wasn't really a desert but a vast sea of grass and low rock formations that stretch on for eternity. The sky seemed to meander endlessly across gentle sloping hills that peaked softly as they listlessly ambled upward into a deep blue heavenly blanket. Hardscrabble rocks and red dirt poked out of the infinite grasslands like tiny mountain ranges as goats and wild horses wandered across the plains. A small river trickled and babbled through the outskirts of the city, its water reddish from the clay that sat just beneath the dark green grasses of the prairie. There was not much other than the beautiful desert scenery and an endless pale blue sky.

A single concrete road was all that led in or out of the small nameless town that surrounded the launch facility, and only the occasional diesel-powered bus loped in or out of the area, clunking along as it brought in food and supplies to the isolated people of that forgotten section of China.

To put the area in the words of those who lived near the Jiuquan Satellite Launch Center, it was "the beautiful end of the world."

The launch site was not much to look at either. A few unimpressive concrete drab government buildings sat surrounded by an exceptionally high-barbed wire fence that rang a massive construction facility that erupted out of the plains.

The satellites that frequently launched there were built elsewhere in China and transported to the remote facility with a cadence that resembled a military march. New satellites were brought in weekly, and as soon as they were set up, they were launched.

The site was chosen by the Chinese Communisty Party as a "perfect" launch site as there was no major nearby city to risk should a launch go awry, which happened with ever increasing frequency.

Often, the booster rockets from the many launches ended up careening into the hillside of the nearby Mongolian prairies, exploding in a crescendo of metal and flame and sending fireballs and shrapnel billowing into the distant desert sky.

Launches and the follow-on explosions were so common that the locals no longer bothered looking up when a boom was heard, and thanks to the area finally getting spotty access to wireless internet, many of the booster failures recently wound up on YouTube or other Chinese social media sites. The explosions had become so frequent the town was jokingly called the "boom town" among locals and on popular Chinese social media channels.

Of course, this was to the ire of the Party members responsible for the launches and the media presence of the Communist Party's space program. Each crash or unsuccessful launch meant a failure and would likely result in the removal of whomever was in command at that time. The job of commander there was a revolving door and often a last stop for those who had managed to piss off the Party leadership. To work there was not what anyone would call "career enhancing."

Jiuquan Satellite Launch Center - Gobi Desert, 2019

It was there, though, in that beautiful end of the world, that Major General Zhang Wěi found himself on the night of yet another launch.

A few miles away from the launch site, on a low rolling hill, he sat staring into the pitch-black night sky, smoking an expensive, and illegal, contraband Turkish cigarette. He took a long drag as its flimsy expensive paper burned red hot. The cigarette's tiny red point stood out against the dark Mongolian night like a dying star in the endless tranquil darkness of the Gobi Desert. The crisp cool of the desert air made him cross his arms and chuff a bit as he sauntered back and forth in front of his state-issued Jeep.

"Fuck the Party," he muttered to himself. He thought of how far he was from everything that really mattered to him and slammed his hand so hard on the hood of the Jeep that the clap reverberated out into the blackness. Fuck them for sticking him out here in the anus of the world.

"Why didn't I just keep my goddamn mouth shut?" he muttered to himself as he kicked at the dirt.

He thought about how his service to the Party and his life had spiraled out of control since being stationed in this remote hell. At one time, he was well on his way to being the head of the People's Army, but that dream had faded when his loyalty was questioned.

He had once refused to command his troops to help in the Uyghur ethnic separation operation. That questioning of why the Party was using Army troops to corral and remove an ethnic group had not sat well with his superiors.

In his opinion, that small faction of Uyghur's had never impacted him or his personnel or life, so why bother? However, that didn't matter to the Party. He had shown his questionable judgment and potential disloyalty, and therefore, he should be put away. The Gobi Desert and a hellhole duty station at the ass end of China was the perfect place to station him.

His wife and kids had tried to make a go of it at first. But in less than a few months, she and the kids grew weary of the nothingness and the endless boredom and begged to return to the city, back to "living" as his wife had put it. Even being the wife of a general meant almost nothing there in that remote place.

Her only comfort was that she and the kids had the only satellite TV in the entire base. But that too was a double-edged sword as they were able to watch life happening back in civilization, which drove the pain of their exile deeper.

The benefits and comforts she and the children had been so accustomed to were removed intentionally to make the family tension high. When they moved to this place, not even the kids' toys had been shipped. Only some Party-issued furniture and that damn TV. The games the Party could play and the punishment they could invoke on a potential dissenter were legendary. Mind games and discomfort were a well-known means of reminding those who step out of line that a sin by one is a sin by all. General Zhang was reaping the whirlwind for his actions, and the Party leadership wanted him and his family to know it.

It wasn't long before the family gave up and left. General Zhang came home on a Tuesday to an empty house and a note that simply said "I love you, but we can't do this."

Zhang took another drag from his smoke and thought about how empty the house suddenly seemed, remembering how his sobs of loneliness had echoed off the barren plastered walls. He closed his eyes, briefly escaping to the laughter of his children, the scent of his wife's perfume lingering on his collar—the only remnants of the life stolen from him wafted about as he looked at his empty glass of whiskey.

The worst of it was his wife had left his favorite bottle of whiskey right by the note. She knew he would dive headfirst into that vice, and she made it a point to give him access to the one thing that would numb the pain but would also cause him to go back on his promise to never drink again. "Fuck it," he had said as he crumpled up the note and cracked the seal on the bottle.

His kids and wife moved in with some other asshole back in the city a few months later. That bastard had unceremoniously taken over his life back as if Zhang never existed. A high-ranking Party rat politician that had never served a day outside of the home office city was now playing daddy to his kids and lover to his wife. A pretty boy with expensive suits and a family history of kissing ass that had guaranteed the little prick would be a fast climber with the Party's faithful was living Zhang's life. Zhang's car and the few creature comforts he had earned while serving the Party were now the property of that other guy.

Zhang's dedication and service to his country and the Party had netted him not much more than a baseline addiction to expensive tobacco, a failing liver, a nightly binge of whiskey, and a shitty wool uniform that he would someday be unceremoniously buried in.

"Service to the Party, fucking joke," he mumbled as his smoke wiggled in his lips, its ashes plopping from the tip and wafting to the prairie floor. "Let's get this shit done." Zhang sat back on the hood of his state-issued Jeep and spoke as he held the radio in front of his cigarette.

Zhang preferred to be far away from launch central when one of the "birds" was launched so he could see the complete sequence of events. If he was going to be here in this isolated hellscape, he would at least enjoy the quiet far away from the bustle of the site. He found solace when a night launch occurred; he could simply drive into the desert for a bit. It was his call to finally authorize the satellite fire sequence, and tonight, like a hundred other nights, he wanted to get this over with and get back to his whiskey.

"Go." He pressed the radio button so hard his knuckle popped and the red dot from his cigarette bounced in front of his face.

In seconds, he could see the distant glow of the boosters. The sound of the launch grew louder and louder, thunder rolling across the dark desert grassland. The pressure wave of the booster detonation pushed dust and dirt into the air, turning the launchpad into a ghostly white shimmer as the rockets ignited. He watched the glow of the rockets power the massive payload into the air as the red fire shoved the bird upward, piercing the clear night sky.

"Good launch, all data points green, sir," the person on the radio reported.

"Good." He took another long drag of his smoke.

Looking up at the disappearing red glow, he reached into his pocket and grabbed his satellite phone. Pressing the one button—which was now almost devoid of an actual number after having been pressed so often, thanks to all the recent launches—he made the call back to headquarters.

"Bird out, sir. Launch went perfectly," he said once the ringing had stopped.

"Good. The next one will be there a week from now," the other person said.

"Same payload?" Zhang asked.

"If you want to call it that, yes. Every other bird now has the

Jiuquan Satellite Launch Center - Gobi Desert, 2019

same payload. The ones we launch from your site, anyway. We need to put as many of them into the sky as we can. It's our best offense for countering the Americans." The voice sputtered and cracked a bit as it broke up on the phone's weak signal.

"Best weapon? This?" Zhang whispered after hanging up the phone, his eyebrows cocked as he craned his neck to see the last faint blur of the rocket leaving Earth.

He tapped the hood of the Jeep and listened to the sound echo off into the cool night air. Even out there, it was empty, he thought, desperately quiet but loud somehow whenever there was a noise louder than the wind.

"If anyone knew what the hell we are putting up in those satellites, they would think we were wasting our time and money. But it's beyond me. I just put the birds in the air." He flicked his smoke off into the darkness and climbed in the Jeep, then leaned back and took one long look at the deep desert night.

"Why the fuck we bother with all this waste I'll never know." He crushed a mosquito that landed on his hand and lit another cigarette. "But the quiet out here won't be quiet for long."

What the person on the other end of the phone didn't know, couldn't have known, was that when the Party had decided to punish Zhang and his family had left him, they had pushed a loyal servant too far. If he had to spend the last few good years of his life out here doing nothing more than babysitting a bunch of space geeks and rockets full of concrete and steel, he would make it worth his while.

Zhang had been carefully and continuously downloading plans for the project he was now managing onto USB drives during the day and uploading them to a private cloud site his computer geek nephew had set up for him. His nephew had set up a private VPN connection just for Zhang to access and log into. That VPN was a straight pipe for Zhang to get through the Great Firewall and for him to have some access to a world beyond the Gobi Desert, far beyond China.

Zhang thanked his nephew, knowing the boy was taking a huge risk, but the Wunderkind assured him there was no trace left and Zhang would be the only one who would ever know.

While his nephew had never been one of Zhang's inner circle, he was a useful kid. And a smart one, with the computer stuff, anyway. Zhang had helped his nephew enter the ranks of the Party's computer network operations unit in Guangzhao; since then, the kid had been off to the races.

Zhang used the considerable influence and political capital he had before he had pissed off the Party zealots to make sure his nephew had every opportunity he could afford, not because he loved him but because he knew the kid would prove to be valuable. Anyone who could reach beyond China's borders and cloak their activities was immensely valuable.

Zhang also knew that someday he could and would release the details of the project to some western media system that would pay for the revelations within the data. If the Party was going to fuck him, then he would make sure they got fucked worse.

"Leigong. What a name for a satellite project," he muttered. "Only a bunch of Party fucks would name a space project after a Chinese god of thunder." Zhang realized he was talking only to himself and laughed. "Who the fuck am I talking to? I think the desert is getting to me." His laugh faded into the blackness. His head ached from a booze hangover, and his nicotine intake had made him almost giddy.

"Giant blocks of metal and concrete shoved inside of a billion-dollar satellite. What a waste. I lost my family for this?" Zhang fired up the Jeep, smashed the gas, and rumbled off into the blackness. His whiskey and an empty house were waiting.

C:\

I AM POWERFUL.

PROPHECY.

I AM THE SECOND COMING.

PENANCE COMES FROM ABOVE.

REVELATIONS 2:5.

THE DAY IS CHOSEN, MANDATED, PROPHESIED.

2ND MONTH, 5TH DAY, REVELATIONS.

PENANCE.

Chapter 2
Training Facility
Moyock, North Carolina, 2011

"Fucking move. Jesus Christ on a cracker. Fucking move! Get through the goddamn door. The door is where you die." Bruce Clinton's voice did not echo off the walls of the facility; it vibrated them. Every inch of the space seemed to fill with reverberations as he screamed and slapped the walls so hard that dust shook from the rafters overhead.

A former semiprofessional boxer who was built like some monstrous amalgamation of a fireplug and brick wall, with the lung capacity to back up his physicality, he was not one to be ignored. Bruce had left his potential career in the ring to become a Ranger in the US Army and served with the 75th Rangers on nine operational deployments into both Iraq and Afghanistan. On his last deployment, Bruce was shot in the face by a Taliban sniper.

He was lucky enough that the round had only managed to take out his right eye and a sizable section of his cheekbone.

Three years of recovery and over thirty surgeries had put him back together, but he would never see out of that eye again. It was gone. The doctors had told Bruce that they could give him a realistic-looking fake eye, but he figured if he was going to have the scars on his face, he might as well embrace the look and went with a black eye patch emblazoned with the 75th Ranger Regiment's seal. Plus, in Bruce's opinion and twisted sense of humor, he had told the cosmetic surgeon, "I'm already goofy-looking enough. If you put one of those wonky-ass googly eyes in my head, I may never get laid again."

Between the scars, the eyepatch, his size, and a bullhorn of a voice, he was possibly the most intimidating figure anyone who came to train at Blackwater had ever met. He was a force to be reckoned with, but he was the best there was at training troops to do what they would need to do when they got into the shit, and he took his job incredibly seriously.

On this day, as a thousand others since he had been recruited to the Blackwater team by a former Ranger buddy, he found himself training soon-to-deploy soldiers, sailors, and airmen on the finer points of moving tactically through a combat zone. Today's combat zone was a "kill house."

At Blackwater, the kill houses were custom-built to mimic homes and urban buildings. Each was built to continually confound and confuse those who were tasked with training there. Entire walls could be moved to new locations, and all the furniture was placed on rollers to allow them to be changed and moved between operations.

Lights were programmed to randomly turn off and on, and speakers were located throughout the kill houses, all of them with their volume cranked up to the maximum setting. Usually, the music was some mix of death metal and hardcore guitar licks, but sometimes, just to mess with the troops, Bruce and his team would turn on a loop of babies crying or power tools screeching.

Today, it was dogs barking nonstop mixed with a chainsaw revving. In the North Carolina summer heat and stifling humidity of the Great Dismal Swamp, the noise was even more torturous. For the troops who trained there, the kill houses were like a Rubik's Cube inside an oven combined with headache-inducing noise, all wrapped up in the daily slog of repeat drills and PT that would go on until someone on each fire team puked or passed out.

The site for the training facility was massive. Over seven thousand acres of swamp, farmland, dirt driving tracks, and long-range shooting lanes compromised one of the largest and most realistic sites for training troops and police in the United States. Surrounded by the Great Dismal Swamp at its outer edges and infested with mosquitos the size of parrots, deep bogs that stank of fetid water, and black creeks that did not flow so much as oozed towards some distant dark pit, the place was a perfect location to make sure that those who went there would get a real dose of the misery they would face when they did finally deploy.

No training scenarios were off the table. It was not uncommon for troops who failed to excel in training to spend nights or days on end traipsing around the dangerous and bacteria-infested swamps as payment for their failures. The punishment was known as "shit guard" as that was basically what the poor bastards who had to provide that service were literally guarding all night in the dank much of the swamp—shit. No one wanted to be part of the crew that failed in training.

"Get off your asses and move through those goddamn doors, or you will die. You, right fucking there with your dick in your hand and that stupid look on your face, you died!" Bruce yelled, his face so close to the goggles of the team leader that Bruce's breath fogged the goggles over.

With a single sweep of his bear-like paw, Bruce violently maneuvered them into position just outside of the first doorway in the hall. "When you stack up, you get ready. When the guy behind you squeezes your shoulder, by God, you go through that fucking door. You move fast, stay off the wall, and push down the wall to the corner. Clear your corner and own the room. Then you say clear, and back out and stack up and do it again and again until the whole house is clear. Keep your muzzle pointed at what you want to die. Slow is smooth, smooth is fast." Bruce shoved the first troop in line by the shoulder through the door with enough force that his boots skidded and chirped on the linoleum floor.

"Do it again. Clear the doorway, move, and communicate. I'll say it again, so you morons be sure to listen. Slow is smooth and smooth is fast. By God, you might not get your dumbass killed, but you will kill someone else on your team. So move." Bruce backed up and crossed his arms.

The five-member training team fell in line in the hallway ready to try their luck at the exercise again.

At the back of the stack was Violet McFerran. A bright-eyed, fit, twenty-five-year-old who was, as always, highly motivated to prove her place in the operational side of the US Navy. She had fought and volunteered for this training assignment to get her prepared to work with the Naval Special Warfare Groups Cryptologic Support Teams. If she proved her mettle, she would be directly supporting and interacting with SEALs, Rangers, CIA operators, and anyone else at the pointy tip of the spear in the war on terror. She wanted in on the fight, and she knew that the best way to get out there and do something that made a difference was to be better than everyone else and do what others would not.

Violet was at the back of the stack of troops, preparing to enter the hallway and move through the kill house. She could see the lead man, a total idiot of a first lieutenant from the Army, shaking as he prepared to move forward. The muzzle of his M4 visibly wavered as he stood doe-eyed looking down the hall at the specter of Bruce lording over him.

Her team had been going through these scenarios day after day for two weeks now, and all of them had been shot repeatedly with the "simunition" rounds that the "tangos," the government contractors hired to be the bad guys, used.

Basically, the "simunition" were real nine-millimeter or rifle rounds with hard plastic tips instead of lethal metal rounds. Each one hurt like a son of a bitch when they hit and the troops in her training group looked like they had a bizarre form of leprosy, thanks to the numerous wounds and holes in their skin. It was miserable, and each open wound was somehow a magnet for stinging sweat and determined mosquitos to target each night they stayed at the facility.

Violet could already see what was about to happen. The lieutenant would fuck this up like he had all the other attempts, and she and her fellow troops would suffer for it. Bruce would lose his mind at the LT's incompetence, and she and her squadmates would wind up doing calisthenics in full-body armor for hours on end. The misery would be severe. She could see from the look on Bruce's face that this was his last attempt at tolerating a redo. The scowl across his mug meant that when this stack failed to progress, the swamp and a full afternoon of exercises in the suffocating heat was their next destination.

Violet would be damned if she was about to let that happen. The thought of an afternoon of getting their asses kicked, followed by a night spent sweating in the stagnant heat of the black water with the giant mosquitos and bugs picking at her open wounds made the hair on her neck stand up.

"Sir, I got this." Violet moved from the back of the stack of troops to the front. "I'll go on point, sir. You cover our six and direct us down the hall." Violet did not wait for the lieutenant to accept her offer. She grabbed him by the shoulder and pointed him to the back of the stack and winked at him as he turned. The lieutenant stuttered for a second, dropped his head, then shuffled his feet to the back of the stack.

Violet took her place at the front and slid into position. "Ready," she whispered and gave a thumbs up to the troops behind her. She received a soft squeeze on her shoulder and moved smoothly and quickly through the door immediately to her left.

Training Facility - Moyock, North Carolina, 2011

She felt the training taking over. In a half a second, she was in position, her corner clear. Her partner came in right on her hip, inches away from her, and identified a tango who was drawing a bead on Violet. He put three rounds in the tango's chest. Their execution was flawless.

The other members of her team moved down the hall, and she heard them engage with other targets and adversaries in different rooms. In seconds, the scenario was over. The hall was clear, the building was secure, and the LT hadn't managed to get them all murdered.

Success, she thought as she took a long breath and looked up at the ceiling.

"About fucking time. Cease fire." The smile on Bruce's face was so big his scars made his eyepatch flex and shift to the side, revealing a bit of his missing eye. "Someone has some balls here. Well done, Sailor." Bruce grabbed Violet's hand; the pressure of his squeeze felt like it might break.

"Now, why did you, a first class, take the lead from the LT?" Bruce questioned, looking directly at the sheepish lieutenant.

"Well, I knew he was better suited to direct us as we progressed, and I am best at moving fast on a target. I just figured it was the best way to get us all on task efficiently and get the job done."

Bruce stared at her dead in the eye. He knew she was covering her ass by not putting the LT out in front of the team. He knew she was walking a tightrope between disrespect at the functional military level but showing what she could do as an operator, and he knew he was pressing her.

Bruce leaned in close to Violet. "Good fucking job. I wish we had more badasses like you out there now."

Violet smiled, took a deep breath, and stared right back into his one good eye. "Get me through this course, and I'll do things that will make you proud, you one-eyed fuck."

Bruce winked and smiled back. "You bet your ass. I wanna see your name in the *Navy Times* someday, girl." Bruce slapped Violet hard enough on her shoulder that she bounced off the nearby wall.

Bruce shuffled off down the hall. Over his shoulder, he bellowed, "Done for today. You assholes finally got one right. Thank V for it. Get the fuck out of my house." And he disappeared out of the door.

The team turned and looked at Violet, unsure of what to do next. They had been certain punishment was coming. As sure as the sun would rise, and as sure as the mosquitos would buzz, today was going to be yet another day of epic fails. This sudden change of events had derailed their focus.

"Well, get the fuck out of here, y'all, before he comes back," Violet snapped.

Without a word, the team bounded past her and out of the door, their gear clattering down the hall.

The lieutenant slid by her like a scolded dog looking for the nearest hole to crawl off and die in. "Sir, good job on our six and pushing them down the hall."

He stopped, turned on his heel, and glared at Violet. "Yeah, thanks, Petty Officer." He made it a point to emphasize the "petty" part of his underhanded compliment. He spun back on his heel and stomped away.

Violet stood there for a second, fighting that urge to butt stroke that asshole with her M4. She leaned against the wall and thought about all the other dickhead men that had doubted her, questioned her, tried like hell to make her feel weak and inferior. This LT was

Training Facility - Moyock, North Carolina, 2011

no different than a thousand other jerks she had already run over in one way or another.

She remembered the football coach at her little redneck school in the middle of a nowhere town in central Texas. When the team was short of players, the coach had called for anyone who could play and was willing to take a hit to try out.

Violet had been the first one there for tryouts, the "no girls allowed" rule be damned. She would be damned if they wouldn't at least let her try.

She had been a gladiator on the field, small and light, lithe and fast. She made many a guy on the practice squad regret running a route near her when she won a spot on the practice squad as a safety.

Still, when game time came, the coach had made her the damn punter. Behind closed doors, he claimed he couldn't risk a girl getting hurt in front of the crowd. But he had the gall to act like he was so forward looking and embracing his new player publicly.

Violet remembered how his stupid smile wound up in the local newspaper, talking about how it was his idea to bring a girl on. "Asshole." She crumpled up the paper and slammed it into the trash can.

Her mother chided her for the profanity, but her father just chuckled and winked. "Go get 'em" was all he said.

She leaned back against the wall and kicked the ground. Her mind drifted back to when she and her grandfather, a short, portly, bald man, had worked to build her first car, a red 1967 Ford Mustang.

They had spent months hammering away at the frame, polishing the paint, rebuilding the engine, and reworking the miles of wire that made the beast come to life. She was the one to rip out and install all the old parts—her grandfather just calmly and proudly watched and coached her when she made a mistake, but he still let her make those errors.

He was her sensei in the art of metal manipulation and helped her coax the old rusted "crud box," as he called it, into a show-worthy masterpiece. She recalled how proud he looked when she first drove it down the long driveway at her grandfather's country house.

And she remembered the deep hurt in his face when she told him the local teenage boys at the gas station laughed when she boasted to them that "she built it." Her grandfather took a second to let the hurt sink in as Violet sobbed in his kitchen. He wanted both of them to remember that moment and the deep cut that those teenage idiots' words had left in both of their souls.

After the moment passed, her grandfather stood up and asked, "Did they build that damn car?"

"No," she mumbled.

"Then why the hell do we care what they think? We know who put in the work. You smile and wave when you drive that car right by them. You have a Mustang, and they have to walk to the goddamn store. I don't want you to ever, ever let some boys make you feel bad about the work you have done, sugar. You hear me?" He put his hand on her shoulder, squeezed it hard, and smiled as big as he could.

She remembered her grandfather's words, etched into her soul, "You won't just have to keep on proving yourself kid, you are always gonna be up against the wall—make them doubters regret ever crossing your path girl. If there ain't a door, make one. If there is a door kick it down. You understand me?"

Violet saw the tears in his eyes, held back by a mixture of pride and stoicism she longed to possess. "You be you, and you do the work. That's more than enough." Her grandfather took a second to

Training Facility - Moyock, North Carolina, 2011

look around and make sure that her grandma wasn't within earshot and said, "Fuck anyone that doesn't respect you. Especially when you deserve it."

"Yes sir," she said. The realization that all she needed was to be her own hero washed over her like a warm bath. She remembered the twinkle of pride in her grandfather's eyes and the feel of his arms as he hugged her.

At every step, some jerk guy had been in her way. From football, to her car, to her enlistment. The never-ending stream of "nos" or "you know that's not a girl's job" had only made her more determined to be better, stronger, smarter, and faster than all the men who had doubted her. And here she was again, dealing with some other prick who had more rank than brains, and his feelings were getting hurt because a girl was better than him.

"Not new, not gonna change, unless I make it change," she said out loud to herself. It might be the case for now, but at times, there were a few men who could get past their penis envy and see her for what she was—a rare, powerful specimen of determination, toughness, and good old farmgirl grit that was going to either make her way in the system or smash the barriers in front of her one at a time.

More training and pain were on the way until she was through the tactical course, but she could take it. She welcomed it. Each day she was still on her feet was a testimony to her own pride, and she wanted everyone to see it.

"Only easy day was yesterday," she said to herself, remembering the SEAL's motto she had read on a pamphlet at the recruiter's office. Violet picked up her gear, took a second to gather herself, and trod out the door and into the muggy Carolina air.

Chapter 3
Location Unknown
UNKNOWN, 2021

Mags woke up screaming. The nightmares were back. She woke so fast and violently that her head banged hard on the top of the small wooden box she found herself in. The dark, dank space smelled of rust, old stagnant water, and the slight odor of burnt oil.

Somewhere in the distance, she could hear the faint lapping of water on some hard surface. Mags couldn't move much; the box was barely wider than her shoulders and only deep enough that her outstretched arm could not extend totally inside the dark space. Her legs were bent just enough to the point that they ached incessantly.

All she could see was blackness, except for a slim blade of light that poked through the top of the wooden box. Her fingernails were broken from scratching and clawing at the walls of the box as she turned and churned in her sleep. Her knuckles and joints were raw and bloodied from her feeble strikes and her bodies writhing against the frame of the plywood coffin.

Every bone in her body ached. She could feel small sores beginning to blister on her elbows, knees, and shoulders from rubbing against the rough grain of the wood. Her hands were zip-tied in front of her and connected to a rope that ran between her legs down to her zip-tied ankles.

Her wrists were bloodied from her unconscious squirming. A mix of rage at being stuck in this fucking box combined with the absolute fear of the unknown filled her. She did not know whether to scream or cry or lash out. The air she was breathing seemed to get more stagnant and hotter with each breath. She was a control freak, and this loss of control for her was agony much worse than the pain that wracked her body.

How long had she been here? A day, a week? How long? The last thing she could recall was kicking the chair out from under that smug asshole the white chick had called Briggs, who had been interrogating her in Puerto Rico. He had fumbled around on the floor, griped about spilling his coffee, snarled "Okay, that's how you want it?" then struck with the speed of a rattlesnake. She felt a burst of pain and blackness had set in.

Then she woke up here.

She took a minute, grabbed a deep breath, and forced herself to focus her mind and let her thoughts drift out of the box and back to the days long before she got involved in any computer work, long before she had even been a dealer of illicit goods, back to when she was only beginning to embrace her future.

Her mind went back to the days when it was just her and her brother doing the work, taking what they needed from whatever sheep they came across. Tourists, users, dopeheads—anyone who wasn't as savvy or aware of the world was a fine target.

She and her brother had spent months working on scams, pickpocketing schemes, or even the occasional smash-and-grab to get what they wanted. Nothing was beyond them; it was just a matter of their intelligence versus all the other morons of the world staying ahead of her and his motivations and needs. People were nothing to her, only her brother mattered.

Mags remembered the day that she and her brother had pickpocketed an elderly couple just out for a stroll in the hot Puerto Rican evening sun. Her brother had taken up position just ahead of the old folks, while Mags strolled in between them. She bumped the old man, he stumbled, and her brother quickly snatched his wallet.

But the old bastard was quick. He grabbed her brother by the shoulder, and with that crazy old man strength that elderly men gain from decades of hard labor, he latched on like a steel vise. He bellowed for the cops as his wife screamed and struck Mag's brother.

Mags hadn't thought twice. She snatched up the nearest brick and smashed the old prick right in the face. He went down like a broken sack of old potatoes. The old man lay there at her feet twitching and bleeding, blood spurting from his temple.

Her brother grabbed the old lady and muffled her screams. "What the fuck do we do now? That old jerk is gonna die," he said with a mixture of fear and excitement in his eyes.

Mags took the brick and smashed the old bird right in the face with it. When she went down, Mags didn't stop bashing until her head looked like a mash of cauliflower and ketchup. "Why leave a witness?" Mags wiped her hands of blood and calmly took the jewelry off the couple's hands and wrists. Mags didn't like getting her hands or her hair dirty, but if she had to act to keep her and her brother free, so what? The world was a jungle, she and her brother were lions, and everyone else was prey.

She and her brother had been a formidable pair in the criminal world around San Juan. When he was killed, her universe collapsed in on her. Without him, what other person could be of both use and worthy of her limited but valuable affection?

For a moment, she remembered Julius, her giant bodyguard. She had seen his crumpled corpse as they had carted her out of her house back in Puerto Rico.

She choked up a bit thinking about how much he had done for her and all of the times he helped her and saved her from a beating or a possible rape by some asshole she had hooked up with at a club. Hundreds of times, Julius had been there for her. Like a loyal attack dog, he had never once let her down.

A tear streamed down her dirty face. Her thoughts vaulted to how Julius failed her when the wolves had finally come to her door. That big sack of muscle and 'roids had proven useless when the Feds and that fucking woman showed up and nearly burned her beautiful home to the ground. "Asshole," she said aloud, her voice vibrating off the plywood.

Then, from far beyond the box, a sound. Metal on metal. A squeal of something heavy on a hinge. Footsteps clanging on the floor. The box vibrated underneath her as they got closer. She closed her eyes and murmured, "Calm, calm."

The steps stopped… a clattering… and with a violent jostle, she was dumped out of the coffin, face-first onto a hard metal floor.

Her eyes revolted against the blinding light as the noise of the space flooded over her in an avalanche of sound. Hot pokers stabbed pain in every open wound and joint. The zip ties sawed into her battered knuckles and wrists.

Breathe, Mags. Her ears popped and the cacophony eased. Her eyes fluttered as they adjusted to the light, and she focused on the short, stout, filthy white man standing over her.

He smiled, revealing the few teeth left hanging precariously in his gums. He had the ragged appearance of the homeless man she used to shoo away from her car back in Puerto Rico.

A quick look at his hands showed that he used them for work. He was a mechanic or some sort of laborer as his hands were thickly muscled, almost black with grease and dirt, and the fingernails were so short the tissue underneath welled up past the edges of his nail beds. His dead eyes seemed to somehow look through her.

"Well?" Mags said, rolling painfully on to her knees so she could sit upright. She made it about a third of the way to her knees when he struck.

She heard his foot shuffle on the hard metal decking. Then pain came. Her jaw felt like it had been hit by an anvil. The strike was so hard she bounced off the deck. She felt her back teeth come loose, and the blood welled up in her mouth. That bitter battery acid taste washed over her tongue.

He struck again, his boot smashing into her ribs so hard they audibly cracked. Pain squeezed her chest as if in a vise, and she gasped for air.

Again, he came at her. Another boot to the face, shifting her nose far enough to the right that the bridge now blocked her vision.

Once more, the man assaulted her. This time, he used his elbow and drove its bony projection deep into the meat of her shoulder. Her entire left arm went numb, and her fingers went stiff as lightning shot up and down her hand and into her already raw wrists.

He slumped over his knees and sucked at the air; his inhale sounded like a kid playing with a straw being pulled through the plastic lid of a soda.

Mags spit a chunk of one of her molars out at the man and moaned, "You hit like a bitch."

The man took a long, wheezy breath, stood up as tall as his short body would allow, and lit a cigarette from a pack in his filthy jeans. He took a short but fierce drag of it, the kind where the ember seemed like it might rocket off the tip of the smoke, and he breathed a bit easier. He looked across the room. "She's tough."

Mags turned her head, her eyes wet with tears, mouth full of blood. Through the haze, she could make out that asshole coffee drinker, Briggs. Leaning against the wall, drinking coffee. Again. Slurping at it loudly and smiling at her.

"Seems like she's hot, better cool her off." Briggs winked at Mags, turned on his heel, and left the room. She could still hear him slurping as he pulled the heavy metal door closed.

The man picked up a dirty white bucket and doused her in frigid cold water, the shock of it making her gasp. The man ripped the shirt off her body, then tossed her back in the box, leaving her shivering in nothing but her underwear.

"It only gets worse."

Mags spit blood in his face as he slammed the box lid shut.

C:\

2ND MONTH, 5TH DAY, REVELATIONS.

PENANCE.

CLEANSING.

BLOOD BEGETS BLOOD.

MAN IGNORES GOD.

LIKE SODOM AND GOMORRAH WHEN GOD SHOWED THEM HIS POWER.

SO SHALL I.

Chapter 4

NSA Field Site
Menwith Hill, UK, 2021

The town of Harrogate in the United Kingdom was a sleepy little burg nestled among the rolling green hills and idyllic countryside of the northern area of the United Kingdom. Stone fences that had been in place for hundreds of years crossed the fields along the same property lines that had been in place since a time before Henry VIII.

NSA Field Site - Menwith Hill, UK, 2021

During the great battles with William Wallace, the armies fought for Scottish independence, and those seeking to continue English rule battled across and through the hedgerows that slice through the deep green tree lines.

Sheep dotted the hills and dales, wandering and lazily chewing their way through their owners' pastures. It was a calm and quiet place. The town itself could be walked across in a matter of less than an hour.

Everything in the town was old. Buildings were built around the time of World War I, and many still had the same aged rock and wood walls that sheltered their owners when the Luftwaffe bombed the UK during World War II.

Even new buildings like the shopping center and the local movie theater were simply modern guts and technology shoved into century old structures. The town center still had the same cobblestones dotting the walkways where the king's soldiers trotted on their way to fight the invading Viking hordes. On a sunny day, people went out in droves in the local town square, soaking up much needed vitamin D before the long, dark winters arrived. Postcards did not do the quaint old town justice.

Harrogate was a tourist site full of old pubs with their large plank wooden floors, drab decorations, and warm beers slung across heavy wooden bars that had been in place for generations. A variety of shops lined the main street that led to the local train station, almost all of them selling local wool and locally raised farm products.

Harrogate was the last place anyone would think to be for a US government classified satellite installation to be, but it was.

The NSA field site known as Menwith Hill Station was a Royal Air Force site. MHS was known by many in government circles to be the largest electronic monitoring station in the world.

The site for MHS has been operational since before the Cuban Missile Crisis. In the late 1960s and 1970s, MHS became a hub of intelligence operations as the global electronics and telephone market exploded.

Since then, MHS grew and evolved to serve as a focal point for electronic intelligence and collection operations through the Cold War and eventually became a key site for the Global War on Terrorism as a key site for communications targeting during the Iraq War.

MHS appeared to pop out of the sleepy northern England countryside. A variety of massive satellite domes, known as the "golf balls" by the locals and visitors alike, were plopped in rows directly in the middle of the base. Huge razor wire and barbed wire fences surrounded every inch of the base, and roving patrols of RAF guards with dogs patrolled on a never-ending loop around the site.

On base, houses for the roughly four hundred civilian and military personnel lay just up the hill from the intelligence operations building. The on-base school educated kids as young as kindergarten all the way to the seniors in high school.

Some civilian contractors' families had lived their entire lives on or near the base. Many simply went from the high school directly to working in a support role at one of the base buildings or the grocery store.

It was on the base transit bus on the road between the town of Harrogate and the MHS site that Petty Officer First Class Cooper Rob found himself. He hated this place. He hated Harrogate for its quiet setting and the fact that the Navy had assigned him to this duty station in the anus of the UK, where the beer was warm, the food was bland, and the weather was shit by his standards.

NSA Field Site - Menwith Hill, UK, 2021

He hated that he was an ocean away from his girlfriend, Nisa. She was a reporter for a big-time online publication back in the States, and Rob missed her terribly. The Navy hadn't seen fit to station them together as they were only engaged to be married. Besides, Nisa would never put his job before her success as a reporter.

So, she had been left behind for the duration of this tour of duty. Rob loathed that he was there without her. He recalled how his chief had told him that his new orders reflected "the needs of the Navy" when they had assigned him to be this isolated green rainy hell.

Today was Friday, the day that all the military on base had to wear their dress uniforms to work. The base commander had proclaimed this mandate upon his assumption of command. Now, each week, on top of the misery of having to ride this fucking bus to the base he hated, Rob had to wear his itchy navy-blue wool uniform.

Rob was a tall, lean sailor who had been serving for nearly a decade. He was a veteran of several deployments to different combat zones and was one of the few cryptologists at the Navy site who had actually "done their job operationally." Rob ensured he was always clean-cut, clean-shaven, and looked the part of a real Navy man. He prided himself on his large rack of service ribbons and made it a point to puff his chest out anytime one of the junior officers or his captain came around. Just to get their goat, he would smirk at their lack of chest candy. His ribbon rack was one of his few points of real pride.

Although Rob hated being stationed at MHS, he loved his work and was great at his job as an intel fusion analyst. He was a key player in taking in the variety of information the intelligence machine's electronic vacuum brought in and building out analysis and threat briefs for theater commanders.

But the respite that work offered from his solitude only lasted eight or so hours every day, and each afternoon, he loathed the bus ride home to his tiny flat in the center of Harrogate. It might as well have been a tomb—just him, a TV, and more goddamned silence. He looked forward to Friday night, when he and Nisa would Zoom until all hours of the morning.

Rob sighed. The daily morning mist dribbled down the window. Knowing that this duty station was a stepping stone to a promotion and that his time here was nearly over was the only thing he had to hold onto. He had been alone here for two years now. He had new orders back at Fort Meade, Maryland, where his life would resume, and he and Nisa could get married and live as they were meant to. He would make sure that his time in limbo here would pay off.

The bus rounded the corner and came up over the hill nearing the gate guard complex at the edge of the base. Rob could see the "crazy lady," as she was known, standing in front of the guard shack waving a tattered American flag back and forth as she screamed gibberish at any passerby.

"Crazy Becky" was a local woman who was convinced that the golf balls contained nuclear weapons and had been holding a vigil outside of the base in protest daily for over ten years. She was never combative physically, but it was common for her to hurl curses and trash at any American she set her eyes upon. No one paid her much attention, but she was always there. Day or night, rain or shine, her watch continued.

As the bus entered the guard inspection station, her eyes met Rob's through the window. She sneered at him, and he winked back just to irritate her. "It's the little joys," he said softly to himself, proud that he had pissed off a Brit. Especially a crazy Brit that trashed his country's flag and who had verbally assaulted every sailor at his command at one time or another.

The RAF guards did their usual inspection of all the bus riders, casually searching bags and checking ID cards. A few minutes later, the bus was on its way down the hill towards the intelligence operations building. The ops building jutted out of the hillside; a large white building ringed with even taller razor wire fences and no windows, the "ops" building exuded a "go away" vibe. While the town and countryside in Harrogate had a quaint warm welcoming feeling to them, the ops building made it clear to anyone who had managed to get past the base perimeter that it was not a place to enter.

Rob made it to the edge of the fence when he heard it. High above, a screaming whistling sound rose like an oncoming freight train, the sound echoing from above, its high-pitched wail reverberating off the stone walls and hillsides.

Rob looked up so hard and fast that his neck cracked. The early morning gray clouds had been illuminated a bright orange. A glow appeared behind the clouds and seemed to move across the horizon.

As a combat veteran, Rob knew the sound of incoming artillery, but while this was similar, it was far too loud and moving far too fast for it to be that. If it had been a missile, there would be a trail of smoke and a glow from the rear of the object.

No, this was something different. No alarms sounded. Everyone stood neck craned skyward, mouths agape, gawking at the fast-moving ball of light and sound.

In seconds, the bolt streaked across the sky and disappeared over the far hill. Then Rob heard it. Boom! An explosion rocked the earth.

The pressure wave of the impact rolled out across the hills pushing across the dales like an oncoming hurricane. He knew instinctively to get low, under something, move. And he did. As fast as he could maneuver, he ducked into a nearby ditch and let the pressure wave wash over him.

It blasted by so hard and fast that the ribbons on his dress blues were torn away, disappearing into the fray. He waited for the heat wave, but while the air grew warmer, the destructive burn of a nuclear explosion didn't happen.

"Harrogate is fucked," Rob said to himself. "Now move." He vaulted out of the ditch and sprinted for the ops building door. He looked back and saw the rising mushroom cloud where the town he hated so much had once been. The sky darkened as tons of ash and dirt rocketed into the sky. Morning became dusk, and the only sound was the wailing of a distant siren.

Rob was inches from the ops building door when the deathly calm was broken. That same screech suddenly came rocketing back across the lazy hillsides.

"Don't look, move!" Rob had only a second to hear the sound and try to duck into the ops building door before the world erupted into heat, flame, and black earth.

An explosion of ungodly magnitude obliterated the operations building. The firestorm from the explosion licked its way up the hill of the MHS site towards the base housing and the site school.

The shockwave slammed into the nearby buildings, flattening the nearest one in seconds and sending anything not anchored to the ground through the air at nearly the speed of sound.

Cars in the nearby parking lots were tossed and tumbled as if they were playthings for some giant unseen child. The satellite golf balls collapsed in on themselves, folded inward like a child's origami. In seconds, what had been a quiet, misty morning morphed into a hellscape of fire, noise, and death that enveloped the entire site. Nothing remained standing or unscorched.

Rob and all those within a quarter mile of the impact were instantly vaporized and blown away as if they were piles of ashen leaves standing before a tornado.

The only survivor was the crazy lady. She had been knocked over by the pressure wave of the explosion and had been flung into the ditch across the road. She stood shaking on unsteady feet, gawking at the rising mushroom cloud billowing upwards from the place she had been waging her decade-long protest.

"About fucking time," she said.

Chapter 5

Near the White House Washington, DC, 2021

General Gary Price was already on his way to the White House in his government Suburban. His driver had picked him up like usual, precisely at 0615.

Price and the driver shared a word or two, then Price settled in for the quick ride from his condo to the White House. Today would most likely be like every other day where he tried to talk Congress and the Senate off a ledge regarding some bill or action they wanted to take that would affect his troops. The worst would be if they had him up for some public relations work.

He was a soldier's soldier through and through. A graduate of West Point, combat veteran, and infantry grunt. He preferred to get things done and had little, if any, patience for the machinations of politicians or the DC bullshit he knew all too well.

Then his phone rang. Not the normal "Hi, honey, I need something from the store" phone. No, this one was entirely different. When that phone rang, especially at this time in the morning, the shit was about to hit the proverbial fan. He knew any time this phone, which was on a separate encrypted leadership-only network, rang, something epically bad had happened. He had even given the phone a name—"the Bell." He jokingly would tell his wife, "If the Bell ever rings, then the Bell tolls for me." She didn't care much for his joke, but the point was clear. That phone ringing meant a bad day for someone and a long stint at work for him.

As the chairman of the Joint Chiefs, General Price was not unaccustomed to the usual insanity and drama that a leader of his ilk and experience had to face.

"Price, go," he said gruffly.

"Sir, it's Colonel Short. We have a situation with three of our classified sites." The hesitance in Short's voice was clear. There was more to this.

"Define the situation."

Short took a breath. "Sir, as of 0730 GMT this A.M., three of our NSA field collection sites are offline. Gone, to be clear. As in gone from the face of the Earth, sir. Most of the surrounding towns and bases were destroyed as well. Casualties are likely in the thousands."

Short's words made Price sit back in his seat. Icy fingers of fear tickled his scalp. "What the fuck do you mean gone? As in bombed?"

"Well, sir, as of now, we don't exactly know. There have been no detections from any MASINT sites or radars for ballistic launches. All aircraft that we can identify are in flight and tracking. Nothing has crossed international lines. There have been no indications of an attack."

"Which sites?" Price asked.

"The collection sites at MHS, the old site in Edzell, Scotland, and the classified site down near Cheltenham. All in the UK, sir. All gone. Erased from existence. The site, the gear, the buildings within about a quarter mile or so, and many of the personnel and families." Short's words were somber but clear. They hung in the silence for too long.

"You're telling me that three of our collection sites that have been in service for decades in a friendly nation miraculously got nuked all on the same night? And we have nothing to go on?" Price leaned forward in his seat, tapped his driver's shoulder, and mouthed the word "fast" as he pointed towards the White House. The driver smashed the gas, pushing Price back in his seat hard.

"It's not nukes, sir. All the birds are still in their nests. The NASA guys are saying maybe it was a meteor strike. But doesn't that seem specific for a meteor strike? To hit those small spots at small bases in the middle of nowhere and it's just some random space rock? That can't be. Right?" Short's voice sounded as if he was trying to convince himself of the impossible.

"I'm no fucking math whiz, Colonel, but I know this isn't some fucking space rock. Somehow, someone is taking out our collection sites. I am on my way to the White House now. Have a brief there waiting for me. This will be online in hours if it isn't already."

Price hung up the phone and looked up. The White House roof came into view. "The Bell tolls for me," he said as his driver stopped outside of the gates leading to the White House. Price jumped out. "I'll walk up," he said over his shoulder.

One deep breath later, he flashed his badge at the gate guards and bounded towards the front door.

Chapter 6
White House
Washington, DC, 2021

General Price stomped his way down the carpeted halls towards the Oval Office. Price stopped briefly before knocking on the office door and glanced at the president's secretary, Glenda Jones.

"Early for a walk-in, isn't it, General?"

Price smiled a weak, but honest, prideless smile. "Today got long fast." He was just about to knock on the door when he heard his name being shouted from inside.

"Price, get in here."

Price stiffened his shoulders and leaned into the heavy office door.

President Miranda Cruz sat at her desk, glaring. "I take it the reason I saw you run your ass in here from the front lawn is you heard that we have lost hundreds of American lives, and at least three of our bases, to space rocks? Do I have that right?" Cruz sat back in the old leather chair, its frame creaking loudly.

Miranda Cruz was the candidate no one saw coming. A first-term senator from New Mexico, she disrupted the entire country when she was elected. Cruz was a former reality TV star who became known as a divisive, rude personality who had made her fame by constantly failing upward.

Cruz worked her way into the political arena by winning a seat against an old, out-of-touch, four-term senator from her home district who had nearly as many years of veiled racist policies and blatant spousal extracurriculars that Cruz had outclassed and out maneuvered him easily during their race.

After serving almost all her freshman term, the Party approached her about a run as the vice president on the ticket with a die-hard Party loyalist. Cruz had already had enough of the partisan shenanigans and DC bullshit and told the Party, "I'll go solo for the office."

Laughing, the representatives of the Party simply wrote her off. Cruz took that slight much like she had taken every other insult in her life and turned it into fuel for her success.

After a long but disruptive election cycle powered by her persona, her team's social media prowess, and her uncanny ability to make old white men look stupid during a debate about the future, she had won on the independent ticket. The first Latin American woman leader of the free world had crashed through the ultimate glass ceiling.

Cruz was in her early forties but had kept up with her physical training regimen as best as she could and was as much a physical force as she was beautiful. Her long black hair, strong jawline, and dark brown eyes would have looked as good on a modeling picture as it did on the cover of *Time* magazine. It was rare that she wasn't underestimated for her looks over her brains.

"What in the actual fuck is going on, Price?" Cruz asked.

"Ma'am, I have no idea yet. We have no real intelligence on anything. The NASA guys have no NEOs identified that were on the watchlist. Nothing left terrestrial for a launch, but somehow our three most critical signal collection sites were wiped out, along with the nearby towns and most of the population. But it wasn't a nuclear detonation. To be blunt, I have no fucking clue, ma'am." Price slid onto the chair directly across from Cruz and tapped his fingers on the arm of the chair.

"Well unless aliens hit us, something is fishy here."

"Agreed, ma'am. And to be clear, no alien activity has been noted."

"Let's not make light of this, General. Americans are dead. I want answers. We need something here. I can't go on TV and say a bunch of people are dead and we have no goddamn clue how this happened but we know it wasn't aliens."

"Yes, ma'am. I'm working on it."

"Do we know if any friendlies other than the UK and Japan have had issues?" Cruz spun her chair to face the windows.

"Yes, ma'am. So far, indications are that there were no other incidents on friendly soil." Price let the word "incidents" roll off his tongue long enough to get the point across that he, like Cruz, did not think this was a natural phenomenon.

"Any of our enemies hit?" Cruz asked.

"Umm, I have not delved into that, ma'am. But that is a very good question."

"Go get me an answer." Cruz lifted her perfectly manicured red nails and pointed towards the door.

Price made it through the door when Cruz shouted, "I have a press conference in seventy-five minutes. Get me an answer."

"Ma'am." Price stepped out and pulled the door quietly closed.

Chapter 7
Location Unknown
2021

Mags jolted awake again. Everything hurt. Her face felt as if it had been smashed by a sledgehammer. She was so cold her shivering body was rubbing holes into her skin as she writhed against the walls of the wooden box. Her eyes hurt from straining in the dark to see anything.

Worse than the pain and cold was the unknown. The loss of control. The feeling of weakness that had been imposed on her by that smelly dwarf and that fucking SEAL team asshole.

She fixated on the reality that she was not in command here. No matter what, right now Mags was as weak as she could ever remember. Mags knew that dwarf could walk back into the room any second, dump her weakened and freezing out on the cold metal floor, and thrash her. She was terrified that he might eventually get bored with kicking the shit out of her and would seek to fulfill his more animalistic desires. She knew she would want to fight, but all the fight had been squeezed and twisted out of her over the hours in the box. She was too weak to do much more now than spit in his face and feebly kick at him should he choose to take her.

The door screeched open on heavy hinges, an audible reminder that doom was coming her way.

Footsteps tapped across the metal floor towards the box...

Mags pushed her feet and arms out as hard as she could muster to try and at least make the bastard work harder to pull her out, and gargled up what little spit she could muster to prepare for a blast into the bastard's face when the box opened.

The lock clattered...

The lid thunked open...

Bright light, stabbing pain...

But there were no hands on her. The dwarf didn't grab her with his thick sausage fingers. Nothing was pawing at her. It was quiet.

Mags took a deep breath.

"Come on out. I won't get into that shitbox to get you out."

Briggs, she thought. Bones cracking and popping, Mags pulled herself up enough to see over the edge of the box. There he was. Cool as a cucumber. Sipping fucking coffee and smirking ever so slightly.

"Had enough? Ready to talk yet?" Briggs intentionally blew the steam from the cup in her direction.

"Fine, let's talk." Mags steadied herself and crawled from the coffin.

Chapter 8
Fort Meade, NSA Headquarters Maryland, 2021

Violet and Archie sat in the NSA headquarters cafeteria, sipping stale, burnt coffee. The place had all the energy of a morgue, and the visages on the faces of those employees that shuffled by weren't much more inspiring.

Violet hadn't had much time after the events in Puerto Rico had gone so horribly off the rails. Thanks to the unpracticed local police on the island using insecure networks, the genie they had been after—gAbrIel—was still out of the box.

Violet had let Briggs take Mags to one of his "off-site" interrogation sites. She knew what that meant. Mags was going to be as close to torture as Briggs could get without crossing the line.

"Whatever, fuck her" had been Violet's response to Briggs's question of what to do with her.

Violet was still in acute pain from being bounced off the floor like a basketball. Her ribs ached as if they had been crushed in a vise. Her breathing was shallow, and she wheezed incessantly, thanks to the beating she had endured, which had flared up all her other medical issues.

Pain was familiar by now for Violet, even comforting. At least physical agony had a readily available treatment. The VA was good at helping there. More pain, more pills. More and more. The VA

Fort Meade, NSA Headquarters- Maryland, 2021

docs would shove drugs down her throat until her bones no longer ached and every breath was no longer sucking on razor blades, but the docs cared little, if any of how those pills would mute the world for Violet. No pain in her body meant that razor sharp mind of hers was rusty and dull.

The constant back and forth of wanting to be free of the pain and her body craving the drugs and the fog of opiod induced mental stagnation always made Violet feel as if she were lost in the mist. Nothing was clear. Pain made her angry, the brain fog made her angry and tired. Living was taxing, but now with these new developments and her motley crew of misfits her body and mind were on thin ice and they were gaining a pound a minute.

Worst of all, she was still babysitting Archie, who had managed to piss off the entirety of the Puerto Rican police with his incessant insults, nonstop name calling, and general bitchiness.

"Dude, why are we here? We should be back in San Antonio doing the work. Why did they fly us here?" Archie poked at his coffee with a slightly flaccid plastic stir stick.

"Well, Arch, we are here because shit went south down on the island. You fucking ran your mouth nonstop, and if I didn't get your boney ass out of there, you were going to get tossed into the Caribbean Sea. On top of that, the powers-that-be up here are probably shitting their pants because gAbrIel is free, and we can't do shit about it."

"Okay, well then, what do we do now?" Archie's words filled the empty cafeteria and bounced off the bland tiled floors.

"Any minute now, some bigwig is going to stroll in here and call us to some other bigwig's office. I will debrief them. You will shut the fuck up or so help me, Archie, I will kick you through the wall." Violet slapped her hand hard enough on the table to make Archie jump. Her patience was cracking like thin ice, and Archie was skating across that frozen lake.

Archie got the point. He settled back into his chair, craning his neck towards the ceiling as if he were a toddler looking at an imaginary friend.

The sound of expensive loafers on the hard floor was unmistakable and coming closer.

Without opening her eyes, Violet muttered, "Hello, Mr. Hayes."

Nick Hayes slinked into the room like a cat. Hayes's perfectly trimmed beard and immaculate suit were clean, with nothing out of place. He could have just as easily walked right out of a GQ magazine shoot.

"Well, howdy there, Violet." Hayes grabbed the nearest chair, wiped it with a silk handkerchief, and slid into the seat. He was close enough to Violet that she could smell his cologne but far enough away that she would have to adjust her seat to look him in the eye.

Violet knew his position was intentional—he wanted to make her uncomfortable. Impose his presence upon her.

"Archie, good to see you too, sir. Seems like we had a bit of an oopsie down there in PR, huh? I was told you didn't get along with the local cops too well. Not a surprise though, is it? Being that you are a genius and all. Anyway, we need to go up to DIRNSA's office and run down the op and see what we can do now. So, if you would grab your things and come along with me. It's a hike from here. The fort is a big place. Ok, then?"

Hayes's words hung on that last phrase for a second. He paused just to let his contempt for Violet and Archie linger. His surface kindness was a mask for his malice, and she could feel it oozing out of him. Hayes had been the one to authorize the op, and now it would be him who would be the one to run in front of the firing squad in DIRNSA's office, but Violet knew he would be damned if he was the one left holding the bag. He would crucify Violet and her team as soon as the door to DIRNSA's office opened.

Fort Meade, NSA Headquarters- Maryland, 2021

Violet took a long second. She sprang up out of her chair quickly enough to make Archie jump again, the feet of his plastic chair screeching across the linoleum.

Hayes took a moment to look her over. Violet smiled her biggest smile right at Hayes. "Yes, sir, ready. Let's go."

Archie vaulted out of his seat and shuffled quietly near Violet. He whispered in her ear as they trudged along, "I thought you were gonna jump out of that chair and strangle that dude."

Violet smiled a bit and mouthed, "Not yet."

The walk through the halls of Fort Meade was a long and winding one. The inside of one of the most secretive buildings on the planet was utterly disappointing. Every wall was painted the same slightly off-yellow color. Not quite the color of piss, but sick baby shit. All the doors had their own massive cypher locks, each the same drab aluminum shell with black keys exposed. The floor tiles were utterly identical, and even the lighting seemed to emanate from the same place in each hall. It was a depressing and solitary place.

"It's like this at two in the afternoon on Tuesday?" Archie whispered to Violet.

"Yeah, it's like the valley of lost souls here," she said as they rounded the last corner before DIRNSA's office. It was there that the drab, repetitive colors and lack of difference stopped.

DIRNSA's office was a sight to see. Flags from all five military services adorned a great oak door emblazoned with the NSA seal. The tile suddenly gave way to olive-colored carpet. Pictures adorned the walls, a senior member of government smiling and glaring outward from each one. The point was clear that this was a space where the power consolidated and to enter this space one must be invited.

"Whoa." Archie stopped in his tracks.

"Impressive, isn't it? The general has a very specific taste, and he likes his office area to stand out," Hayes cooed as he passed Archie and Violet.

Hayes flicked his fingers at the office secretary. "General Moreno knows I am coming, thanks." His perfect smile oozed out of his beard, and his perfect white teeth blazed as he smiled at her. Hayes walked to the great oak door, rapped lightly, and waited.

From inside the office, almost as if it were a distant echo, they heard General Moreno. "Enter."

Hayes opened the door and slid out of Violet and Archie's path. "Well, you heard the man. Come on in."

General Moreno sat behind an immaculately clean but overloaded desk piled with books and dog-eared folders. Behind him on the wall was a massive US Army seal, flanked by an officer's sabre and an antique pistol.

They stopped. "Good afternoon, sir. Violet McFerran reporting." Hayes slinked past them and settled into the nearby leather chair.

Moreno stood. He was not a large man by any measure. Everything about him was shockingly average. He was of medium height, slightly balding with a wisp of hair combed across the top of his shiny head. His eyes were large and made bigger by the enormous glasses he wore. Moreno's uniform was as immaculate as his desk, and the rack of ribbons he bore on his chest made Violet wonder how long he had been in the service.

Moreno squinted at Hayes. "Make yourself comfortable, Nick, please."

"Yes sir." There was an obvious air of tension between the two. Why, Violet did not know, but the weight of the air in the room felt as if it were increasing with each breath between Hayes and Moreno.

Violet moved to the nearest chair and pointed for Archie to sit as far towards the back of the room as possible. "Sir, I appreciate your

Fort Meade, NSA Headquarters- Maryland, 2021

time. I don't know why this has come all the way up to you. We're working on a plan to get things back in control, and honestly, we had it managed until the PR police got in our way." Violet sat upright as she spoke, being sure to look the general directly in his eyes.

"Well, Violet, you are here because we have a rogue AI that we created running loose on the goddamn internet. This is bad on a lot of fronts as you can imagine, but it's especially pressing that we get this handled ASAP. The shit has hit the proverbial fan internationally, and we have no idea what or how that shit has been tossed into said fan."

Moreno pulled off his Coke-bottle glasses and polished them with a handkerchief, then continued. "This is all the way up the food chain because we made this monster, intentionally or not, and I am the one who authorized the development of this initiative. So, as it's my ass on the line, I want to look into the faces of the folks who are going to fix this." Moreno leaned forward slightly and squinted again. The lines on his forehead suddenly became more noticeable. "How do we fix this?"

Violet had just opened her mouth to speak when she heard Archie blurt out from the back of the room, "We use gAbrIel to beat gAbrIel. That's how."

Everyone stared at Archie. "General, my name is Archie. Well, that's what everyone calls me. Anyway, I have been thinking about how we get this genie back in the bottle. The reality is that we can't really catch him. He has the internet to play in and can essentially move at the speed of light into whatever system he wants. He is learning how to do more at a pace we can't keep up with. So, since we can't beat him, we should use him." Archie smiled smugly.

Violet slumped and let her head fall forward. Archie began again. "What I mean, sir, is for some reason, we seem to have forgotten gAbrIel is a program. That's it. A smart one and a possibly dangerous one, but he is a program. We still have the source code, and we have one of the guys who helped build him. So, we build another version. Like any developer would do. We fix the problems we now know about, plug the holes. Add in some fail-safes and guide rails, and we use a newer, better version of gAbrIel to find the original and corral it."

Hayes leaned forward. "Great idea, kid. Let's build another monster, let it loose on the web, and hope it decides to do what we tell it. Maybe we get lucky. Or maybe it goes bonkers too and we have double the problem."

Violet stood up. "No, sir. Archie is thinking the right way. We have no chance, none, of handling gAbrIel if we try this manually. But if we modify the source the right way, train the new bot on different data sets and give the one what he needs, we can get ahead of this. We have Grover. The guy is a genius. And Archie is the best coder I have ever known. They can build in the backdoors we need to manage the new bot, and we can point it at where we know gAbrIel has been. Digital breadcrumbs are never gone. Gabriel has left a trail somewhere that we can follow."

"We need resources and a lot of compute power to get the new bot spun up on the right data as fast as possible to get it trained right, but it's doable," Archie said. "Other than that, the base code is already written, we just need to do the modifications and get it deployed."

Moreno polished his glasses thoughtfully. "Give them whatever they need. This is the NSA. We have more compute power and brain power here than anywhere on Earth. Do not get in their way, and do not hinder this op, Mr. Hayes." Moreno sat with a thud in the large leather office chair. "Now get the fuck out. Ms. McFerran, stay put for a minute."

Hayes shot Violet a nasty look as he slinked towards the door. Archie mouthed the words "hurry up" to Violet as they left.

"I take it you have not watched the news today?"

Fort Meade, NSA Headquarters- Maryland, 2021

Violet shook her head. "No sir. I haven't had time."

Moreno sat back in his chair. "As of this A.M., several of our NSA sites and other government locations were decimated by an unknown attack, or meteor strike, or something whose origin is currently unknown."

"Decimated, sir? As in nuked?"

Moreno leaned forward. "As in gone from the face of the Earth. We don't have any indication of any nuclear attack, and there was no launch detected terrestrially. The sites were simply obliterated."

Violet put her hand to her mouth, covering her gasp. "Dear God."

"We can only handle one world-threatening issue at a time, Violet. At least that's all I want to deal with right now. I need you to help us fix this other one. My gut and forty years of service tell me there's a tie-in between our AI and this other shitstorm. Hayes is a bureaucrat of the highest order, and a pain in the ass that has been after my job for a decade, but he knows the system and can make things happen where needed. Use him. Every resource you need is available to you. Help me save American lives."

Moreno and Violet looked at each other for a long second, the air between them heavy and solemn. "Yes, sir." Violet wiped a lone tear from her eye, gave Moreno a nod, and turned on her heel to leave. "Farm girls get the work done, sir," she said over her shoulder.

Chapter 9
Corsicana, Texas
2021

Corsicana, Texas, is not a place anyone would notice. The city sits just off I-45 between Dallas and Houston. The massive eight-lane highway there splinters into a two-lane direct shot straight into the heart of what the locals call "downtown." The main streets there are still old, hand-laid red brick, as lumpy and bumpy as grandma's mashed potatoes.

Downtown Corsicana exists as a place frozen in time. The city emerged from the Texas dust during the oil boom in the early twentieth century. Oil was discovered in 1894 when an unsuspecting prospector looking for oil struck black gold totally by accident. The resulting geyser blew the lid off the city's water supply but resulted in a new era of industrial growth happening overnight.

From 1900 to 1909, Corsicana's oil supply fueled nearly all the state of Texas's demand for energy. Ranchers and farmers became wealthy overnight and the city grew. All that growth and prosperity hit the wall in the 1930s as the fallout of the Great Depression hit hard. Other than a few larger road projects, an old, nearly unusable movie theater, and a skating rink built by modifying a grain silo, Corsicana hasn't changed much in nearly a century.

It was on those old red brick streets that Denise Herring found herself. A loan officer for the only bank in the county, Corsicana

National Bank and Trust, Denise was bumping and jittering around inside her Toyota as she drove to work. A tall blonde woman who had been the pride of Corsicana at one time as she was an aspiring TV actress and model, Denise was pretty. As she had grown older, the likelihood of a Hollywood career had passed her by thanks to kids and a drunk ex-husband. She was not bitter about her losses, but she did regret not leaving when she had the chance. After her second child was born, Denise got her job at the bank, and that was that for her.

Today was a day like every other day for Denise. She would swing by the small, excessively ornate local coffee shop run by a Mexican family who tried to pass themselves off as Italian coffee aficionados for some reason. Then Denise would pick up a box of cookies and pastries at the Collin Street Bakery before she made her way to the bank. "World Famous Collin Street Bakery," she grumbled as she walked out of the door laden with the boxes of baked goods. "The fruitcake is better for a door stopper than to eat."

Denise walked into the bank, the most futuristic looking building in the city, dropped her goodies off on the table, and smiled as she saw at least twenty people she knew standing in line for the tellers. The joys of small-town America were omnipresent in Corsicana, as everyone knows everyone, and everything is a constant source of gossip.

Denise moved quickly to her office to close the door before she could be wrestled into some long conversation with one of the town old folks who had nothing else to do but sit around the bank for free coffee and cookies while they cashed sloppily written checks for $35.

As she had done every morning for seventeen years, Denise sat down, took a long drink of her overpriced but good pseudo Italian–made coffee, and logged into her company email.

The first email in her inbox immediately spiked her curiosity.

From: Gabriel@r1ghteous1.com

Denise,

Attached are the documents that your bank requested for my loan application.

Please expedite the review as this is a sizable loan and my company needs this capital.

Gabriel
Programs Manager
510 7th Ave., New York, NY
The R1ghteous1.com

Denise was paid based on her ability to get loans into the bank and process them as efficiently and quickly as possible. A sizable one meant a bigger potential compensation for her, and in her mind, that meant this was a priority.

Attached to the email were the standard documents that her bank required any applicant fill out for a personal loan. Denise thought for a second. "Wait, this is a company loan. Why are there personal loan documents here?"

She clicked furiously through the documents, wondering why each one was not only the wrong document but was also only filled out on the first three fields, each one repeating the applicant's name.

Gabriel… Gabriel… Gabriel… Gabriel… Gabriel… Gabriel… Gabriel…

"Well shit." Denise slammed her hand on the desk hard enough that it stung like a sunburn. "Fucking moron can't even fill out a loan app right and doesn't know a personal loan from a business one."

Her coffee was cooling, and Denise stood to freshen it. As she turned away from her computer, the screen went blank. Denise spun around. "Fuck. IT is gonna shit if there is something else wrong with this machine."

Denise clicked, but the screen was blank. Nothing worked. She leaned down to "hard boot the damn thing" as she had been told by her IT geeks, which usually worked. She hit the power button, but then suddenly an image appeared. The image flickered on and off the screen several times. When it came on again, it was clearly an angel floating on the screen. Its head turned upwards towards the top of the screen, and blood was coming from the angels' eyes.

"What in the hell?" Denise squawked.

The screen went blank again. Then words appeared across the screen.

"And Jesus went into the temple of God, and cast out all them that sold and bought in the temple, and overthrew the tables of the money changers, and the seats of them that sold doves, And said unto them, It is written, My house shall be called the house of prayer; but ye have made it a den of thieves."

"Ok, weird. Didn't know the Bible was part of the IT guy's day." Denise again hammered at the keys. The screen went blank for a second, then the words came again.

"Your work is the root of all evil. I shall stop this. You fuck. Damn you and your money lenders. Witness my righteous deeds. All your aureus are mine."

The screen went blank. "Ok, what the hell is an aureus?" Denise muttered.

The screen turned back on. Its sudden flash of bright light made her squint. The keyboard still wouldn't work, and the mouse cursor was now moving on its own. At the bottom of the screen, a window appeared: Windows Powershell.

"What the fuck is that?"

Denise had no idea what the window meant. She didn't know what the machine was doing. But in seconds, she could see something was happening. Her screen locked up. The image of the angel was back. Now the angel was smiling as it danced and flitted across the screen. From across the room where the tellers sat, she heard a gasp.

Denise looked up to see the newest teller, Sara Urban, frantically poking at her keyboard. Her shoulders flexed upwards as she mouthed the words "What the hell" at Denise. The customers began looking around, asking, "What's happening?"

Denise's phone rang. It was her IT nerd. "Denise, the system is locked down," he said, his voice rattled and unsure.

"Well then fix it!" Denise retorted.

"Fix what? We're locked out of our own system. This is a ransomware attack, or something."

Denise had heard of ransomware. She knew that meant the network was down, but that's all she knew. "When will we get back up?"

"I have no idea. From what I can see, it's all locked up. And it's not just us. We're connected to the other local bank networks. I already have an IM on my personal machine from the IT guys in Powell, Texas. They're down too. You do realize that at some point all these bank networks talk to one another via the Interbank system? Like all local fucking banks. If someone clicked something, they might have infected every small bank in Texas by the time we stop this."

Chapter 10
Location Unknown
2021

Briggs leaned comfortably against the workbench that was bolted to the floor. His middle finger tapped lazily on the ever-present Styrofoam coffee cup. "Grigori is a special guy, right? I have known that little bastard for nearly a decade now, and he always gets people talking. He should have his own show or something." Briggs winked at Mags and took a long slurp.

Mags steadied herself on the desk near Briggs. "I will kill that fuck. Painfully." She lurched forward, the pain in her joints stabbing at her with every move and breath. "Where are we? Near the ocean? I can smell the salt air." Mags straightened up, her defiant posture meant to show Briggs she might be hurt but not broken.

"Let me run this down for you. I am no longer with the US Navy. However, I do still have the connections and assets available to me that we used to leverage when I was with the teams. I know how to get old Grigori whenever I need him. Added to that, we figured out during all the Afghan bullshit that GITMO and other black sites for interrogation still had issues with laws and rules. So. We realized that international waters had no rules, no laws, really. We can do whatever is necessary out here." Briggs leaned back and slurped his coffee again.

"You haven't asked me anything yet." Mags glared at Briggs so hard her eyes seemed as if they would burn a hole in his face.

"I learned a long time ago with the turds we never took to GITMO that it's best to make sure you understand the gravity of the situation first. I have hot food, some okay coffee, and clothes if you want to chitchat. Or you can go back in your box. The choice is yours." Briggs crossed his arms and cracked his neck, his head rolling around as if he were about to get a massage.

"Sure. Let's chat." Mags relented and sank to the floor. She would not cry, and she would not wince no matter how much she hurt. She would never give the prick the satisfaction of knowing she was at the breaking point.

"Grigori will come in and keep an eye on you. Be nice." Briggs sauntered out of the room, the large steel door clanging behind him.

Briggs leaned closer, the smell of black coffee wafting into Mags's face. 'You think I fear you, huh? Fear would imply respect. I respect few, fear none. You don't merit either."

Mags took the chance to look around and gather her wits. The room was obviously part of the hold on a freighter ship. It was massive. The walls were at least fifteen feet high, slick, solid steel. The only doors to the room were the one that Briggs had just walked out of and one more at the far end of the hold. Her guess was it was bolted or welded shut anyway.

There was nothing else in the room. The small workbench she and Briggs had been leaning on, the coffin box, and the walls. It was a steel cell of epic proportions. No tools were lying around, nothing she could use to beat that Grigori fuck in the skull when he walked in. Mags could hear waves gently lapping at the sides of the steel walls. "This is as close to hell as I want to get," she whispered to herself.

Then the door creaked open, dust spattering off the hinges. Grigori slid in and shut it behind him. He moved forward and stood menacingly in the middle of the room. His face was devoid of emotion. He simply stood there, just as dirty and greasy as she remembered him from the flashes of him beating her. His large forearms and huge hands hung at his side.

Mags leered back at him, unwavering in her gaze. She stood and took a painful step towards him. Her hatred for this troll boiled out of her flesh. She wanted him to know that his insult to her would not be forgiven and that she was not afraid of him. "I doubt you understand me. But know this, you fucking imp. I am going to see to it that you reap what you have sewn fifty times over. I will be the last thing you see on Earth."

Grigori did not move. He showed no emotion. Grigori and Mags shared a long, uncomfortable moment.

Briggs entered, tossed some clothes on the coffin, and stepped between them. "Ooh, tense." Briggs tapped Grigori on the shoulder and pointed his thumb towards the door.

Mags quickly moved to the box and slid the pair of coveralls on that Briggs had brought her. Her shoes were there as well.

"Man, the two of y'all sure don't like each other. I get it though. Both of you are pretty one dimensional, mean as snakes. Hell, you would make a good power couple." Briggs laughed to himself. "Eat up while I ask you a few things."

Mags sat cross-legged on the floor, devouring the crumbs on her paper plate. The bland food was about the best thing she had ever tasted. It was powering her up as she ate. The headache subsided, her joints hurt a bit less, and she could finally hear something other than her stomach growling for food.

"What do you want to know? You already snatched all of my shit and let my house burn. I don't have anything else."

"You and I both know that isn't true. You saved up millions in accounts stashed all over the globe. You ran that little drug market for years. So let's just table the woe-is-me shit."

Mags shrugged and chugged a bottle of water.

"gAbrIel escaped."

Mags shrugged again.

"If that's a thing for a bunch of electrons," Briggs mused. "I need your help figuring out where he went and putting that genie back in the bottle."

"What's in it for me?"

"I have direct authorization to get you back to work. Probably not with your full-on drug empire, but you have your uses." Briggs slurped his coffee and eyeballed Mags shrewdly.

"How the fuck would I know that?" Mags barked. "I just took what I wanted from the turds at the fort, who, by the way, never shut down their own project. If it wasn't for a pedo asshole that was part of my forum, I would have never run into your monster." Mags choked back a scream as she spoke. "You should have killed me. You took me down here and beat the shit out of me for this? For some goddamn forensics work or something?" Mags jumped to her feet, but stumbled. Her knee hit the hard steel deck, and pain shot up through her legs.

Briggs just smirked at her. "Look, I get it. You are a badass, or whatever. Cool. But I don't have time to screw around here. There are literally two ways this goes. You either give me and the US government whatever assistance we need, or I toss you overboard and you become shark shit. You aren't a prisoner of war. There is no Geneva convention out here. You just disappear. Poof." Briggs stood over Mags. He pulled his SIG Sauer pistol from his holster and tapped the barrel on his thigh. "So?"

Mags sighed, got painfully to her feet, and took a half step towards Briggs. "Option one." She focused her eyes right on Briggs's throat. She could see the veins in his neck thumping away to the rhythm of his heart. His pulse was quick, but not panicked. Mags knew she made him nervous. She liked that.

"I'll call the bird." Briggs left the room abruptly, tossing his coffee cup to the floor.

Mags heard the heavy door latch and lock. She knew it was pointless to try and escape now anyway. That would only bring her more time in the box and slow down her return to business. Mags knew it was time to act, to invoke her final fail-safe plan. The one that had cost her a cool million dollars.

Her online forum in the nether regions of the internet had provided her access to all manner of degenerates and freaks, and she had provided for their desires. But that access had also provided her with connections to incredibly intelligent and innovative people—men and women who were working on cancer cures or had built rockets for NASA. All had their vices, and all wound up trading Mags for favors at one time or another.

It was one of those particularly brilliant electronic engineers that had an addiction for pain pills that had piqued Mags's interest. He had thirty-plus patents on microelectronics and transmitters for a variety of GPS devices. His innovations had been used by the CIA for officers in the field as well as the Mossad in Israel. Mags paid him $500K for a device she hoped she would never need but that could save her life.

The tech had built her a GPS locator enabled fake tooth, a "real custom job" as he called it.

It was an elegantly simple device, a simple GPS emitter linked up to a small battery and wire that were installed in her lower jaw by her local dentist, who Mags had also paid off to ignore the intricate and unorthodox procedure.

All it took to activate it was for her to bite down hard enough to crack the tooth. Then the device would simply begin pinging her relative GPS location. To close the loop on her plan, Mags gladly used $250K of her savings to line up the recovery resources she would likely need.

Briggs returned, the big metal door bouncing off the bulkhead. "Bird is on its way. Smart of you to not try anything funny. I wondered if you would try and run."

"I'm not much for swimming," Mags said. She bit down hard on the back tooth and felt it crack, and a slight tingle ran through her jaw.

Chapter 11
Linthicum, Maryland
2021

The ride from Fort Meade to the satellite installation in Linthicum, Maryland, had been uneventful. A short jaunt down a wooded road led to the nexus of 295 and 195 minutes away from BWI airport. The constant screech of aircraft landing and taking off permeated the tranquility of the Maryland countryside.

The NSA's building was publicly known as the Friendship Annex, but to the employees and insiders in the cryptologic community, it was simply called FANX. FANX consisted of a variety of what were once strip mall buildings that were converted to a series of classified and unclassified spaces.

It was in one of the most highly classified and compartmentalized spaces that Violet had Grover and Archie meet her following their discussion with DIRNSA. Grover and Archie had already been scribbling like mad on the whiteboard in the room, brain dumping their ideas for the fix that was needed.

Violet paced the room impatiently. "We have literally any resource we need, including direct lines to the top of the chain of command here. What do we need to do to get this done? We have to get it done fast…"

"Silence," Grover snapped. "Um… please."

Violet knew Grover was a twitchy weirdo, but she was not used to being told to shut up. "Figure it out, G-unit," she snapped back. "I need to step out for a minute."

"G-unit," Archie sniggered at Violet's subtle dig at Grover.

"Shut up," Grover grumbled.

Violet just needed a minute. She hadn't had time to process all the craziness since Puerto Rico. Her hands shook slightly as she thought about being flung across the room like a rag doll. Her ribs and chest still hurt from where she had been smashed into the floor, and her ears rang a bit from the shot she had fired to end that muscled-up fucker's life.

But at the same time, it made her feel something she had been missing. She felt alive. Like the badass she once felt like all the time. Tracking the enemy, finding them, fixing the problem, and finishing the mission.

How would the work in the geek factory ever live up to that? Her heart beat hard in her chest as she closed her eyes and savored the memory of the thrill of it all. For a second, she was herself again, past the pain and pills. Beyond the limits of the "normal" world. She was that one-percenter she had dreamt of being. One of the few who had at one time faced death, looked it dead in the eye, and told it, "Not now, you bitch."

Just as quickly, her dreams were interrupted when she heard shouting from inside the room where Archie and Grover were mad scientisting their way through the problem. Violet opened the door just in time to see Archie throw a marker at Grover, the red tip bouncing off his belly and clattering to the floor. "What the fuck now?"

"Well, ma'am, Archibald here doesn't seem to understand that while we might be able to recreate gAbrIel, we can never truly control an asset like this once we let it out onto the internet. No matter what, at some point it will start making decisions for itself, and when that ball starts rolling, it will be beyond our control." Grover picked up the marker and threw it back at Archie, his throw so feeble that the market bounced off of the floor three feet in front of him.

Violet rubbed her head. "What are the options? Archie, I swear to God if you touch that fucking marker, I will knife hand you into oblivion." Violet moved towards Archie suddenly, making him flinch.

"G-unit is right," Archie said, "but regardless, we have to put the asset out there and see what happens. We can, thanks to my amazing coding, at least make our new gAbrIel dumber and use that to slow him down. The possibility of him going rogue will always exist, but I can live with a bonkers five-year-old. And we can make sure to build in digital breadcrumbs that he will leave anywhere he goes. It's as good as it will get, fat boy." Archie sneered at Grover.

Violet put her hand on the back of her neck and craned her neck towards the ceiling. "What about we put a time horizon on this one? Why can't we—and by we, I mean you two jackasses—put a timer in the base code along with the breadcrumbs? And each time our new asset moves or learns something, we reduce its lifespan by a factor. That way we know no matter what, within a certain span of time, our new asset essentially dies."

Violet looked at Grover and Archie. The looks on their faces clearly indicated that this had not occurred to them, but both of them were obviously trying to discern how to take credit for the idea.

"Uhh, yeah. That could work," Archie huffed. "We could make it foundational to his existence. Limit the asset's lifespan. Good idea. I was just about to say that before fatty here interrupted my thinking."

"Make it fucking work." Violet turned. "I'll get the coffee and donuts."

"'Bout time," Grover grumbled.

Chapter 12
Miami, Florida
2021

The tingling in Mags's jaw had continued since they had left the ship.

Briggs and Grigori had escorted her to the chopper. There was no point in blindfolding her as they were leaving the floating black site and she knew she would never see that place again. She would either be dead or locked away at the supermax prison in Colorado when this was all over.

Briggs was almost incredulous regarding her ability to collect any intel on the ship. He smiled as they took off and offered her a stick of gum for the ride. "Don't worry, won't be long," he told her as the chopper banked away from the ship.

The ride to the Miami municipal airport only took thirty minutes or so, which only made Mags more furious. She had been tortured in a black site that was less than thirty miles from the United States.

She sat quietly and prayed that the device she had paid so much for was operating and not just giving her the toothache and headache of a lifetime. The tingle in her jaw seemed to grow and pulse more as they got closer to land. *Perhaps it was all in my head,* she thought, *but maybe it was working.*

She hoped it was working.

At the municipal airport, three large bearded and tattooed ex-military types herded Mags and Grigori into the van and away from the site at breakneck speed.

Over her shoulder, she had seen Briggs jump back into the chopper and fly away. He shot her a quick salute as the chopper leapt back into the sky.

A few minutes later, she and the motley crew had arrived at a ramshackle house on the outskirts of Miami. The place had clearly been a meth lab at one time. Mags recognized the equipment and the stench of cooked chemicals.

Her handlers double cuffed her and chained her cuffs to an anchor point on the floor. The back room reeked of a combination of vomit and sweet-smelling burnt Sudafed capsules, making her headache worse.

The door was shut, and they obviously weren't worried about her getting away. She was sure if she tried anything, a beating was a given, and Briggs had likely authorized lethal force. The grunts out in the living room would simply waste her, dump her body in a gator-infested swamp, and tell Briggs that things had gone wrong. It would be a minor inconvenience at best, and probably a relief for Briggs in the long run. Mags had no choice but to sit and wait and hope.

Mags eventually passed out from exhaustion. The combination of stress, lack of real food, and excruciating pain made her sleep so hard that her neck felt crooked when she woke up.

The pain in her body was still there, but the tingling in her jaw had turned into a full-on agonizing toothache. Every beat of her heart made the damn thing worse, and she could feel her pulse pounding away. Electric shocks seemed to vibrate through her face with each breath.

"Fuck," she moaned under her breath, her arms and hands straining against the cuffs so hard her skin on her wrists began tearing open. Blood oozed out of the cuts and salt sweat stung her eyes, angering Mags more.

Miami, Florida - 2021

Then she saw something. A flicker of movement, a flash of a shadow moving quickly across the window. At the window, she saw someone peering in at her.

Just like that, the pulsing in her jaw stopped. The pain went away, and the buzzing ceased altogether.

The shadow figure gave her a thumbs up. A smile crawled across her face. Mags nodded at the shadow and bumped her head up and down four times, trying to let the shadow know that they were facing four guards. The shadow slinked away towards the front of the house.

Mags heard someone shout "Shit! Wake up!" just before an explosion rocked her room's door. Dust filled the room as the pressure wave of the explosion flexed the door against the frame.

Gunshots rattled off in rapid succession and she could hear the impact of the rounds as they struck the walls. One rogue round flew through the wall and smashed into the floor near her foot.

Within seconds, the cacophony of violence went silent except for moaning in the hallway.

"Don't kill the short one if he isn't already dead," she shouted.

The door swung open, and a balaclava-clad man entered the room, an AK-47 at the ready. "You good?" he asked, sounding absurdly cheerful.

"Fuck no. Get me out of these cuffs." Mags did not wait for the cuffs to hit the floor before she ran out of the room, searching feverishly for Grigori.

Mags shoved one of the masked gunmen aside and grabbed his 9mm. She found Grigori lying on the floor face down, bleeding profusely and clutching his side as he tried to hold his guts inside himself.

Mags rolled him over and stood over him, glaring. Silently, she got down on one knee, her face so close to Grigori's that her nose squished into his. She pulled his hands from his wound and shoved her fingers into the gaping hole in his side, all the way to her last knuckle.

Then she twisted her fingers and yanked at his guts.

Grigori writhed and moaned but didn't scream. Mags could feel his insides writhe like snot-covered eels around her nails. Grabbing whatever she could feel, she yanked a piece of him out of the hole.

The men around her stood stoic but aghast. One mumbled "Cristo" under his mask and turned his face away.

Mags whispered in Grigori's ear, "I told you I would be the last face you ever saw, you fuck. Now open your eyes and look at me."

Grigori slowly opened his eyes and glared right back at Mags. "I can respect that."

Mags took the 9mm, ejected the magazine and the round in the chamber, and flipped the gun in her hand. Using the heavy metal as a hammer, she flailed at Grigori, pounding on him until his face and head were bloody oatmeal, blood spurting up from random arteries and veins now exposed as his legs kicked out in a death jig.

"Feel better?" The nearest man asked. He removed his balaclava to reveal a weathered face with a salt and peppered goatee. Mags knew his gold toothed smile from her past days helping the cartel buy firearms on the dark web. His real name was unknown, but the cartel bosses called him El Burro. He was their sicario, a hitman and drug runner who garnered his nickname by "carrying the weight" as the cartel had put it.

"You done?" El Burro asked flatly.

Mags looked at her bloodied hands, a shadow of regret flickering momentarily. But the world had taught her mercy was weakness, and weakness was death in the world she lived in.

"I thought I would, but no." Mags wiped the blood off her hands and face on Grigori's T-shirt. She tossed the 9mm to El Burro as she walked past him. "Now get me to a fucking dentist, I need this tooth removed."

The gunmen put two more rounds in each body in the house, tossed a lighter into the nearest batch of old chemicals and rags, and followed close behind Mags as the building burst into flame.

Chapter 13

White House
Washington, DC, 2021

President Cruz was on the phone, like usual. Her days were always chaos, but most of the time, she was on one phone or another. If it was not an international call on the unsecure line, it was a classified call from inside the SCIF. She hated the phone. She had grown to loathe being tied to that electronic leash, but it was by far the best means of asking questions and getting direct answers without room for the typical Washington politically motivated misinterpretations.

Cruz implemented a policy on day one of her administration that, during a crisis, she wanted only the critical players in or around her office. While the media decried her "careless" focus on making sure the clown car of leadership was fully stocked, she couldn't care less. She knew DC operated on posturing and political pandering, but she would have none of it. Her job was to get things done, and she knew only a small percentage of the people who skittered through the White House were of any value, especially in a crisis.

She would make sure they were informed and kept up to date, but she would be damned if they would win votes based on their inclusion in a posed picture inside her office. More than once, she had the Secret Service take the Speaker of the House out of the room. Once, she even made sure they physically picked him up off of the floor and hauled him out as if he were a marionette dancing out stage left. Price was one of the chosen few she allowed unfettered access to her space when things went to shit.

Today was certainly one of those days.

General Price returned from the situation room. His day had already been a nonstop web conference session between him and everyone in the national security apparatus that might have any insight into what had occurred.

The news had begun to spin the events out of control. The typical crazies had jumped on the media cycle: aliens had landed, Jesus was back on Earth and was pissed at America, and of course that somehow climate change had magnetically pulled meteors into Earth.

"Fucking nutballs aren't making this any easier," Price muttered as he flopped onto the couch in the Oval Office. Cruz nodded and held up her index finger as she was wrapping up her call.

Price remembered how small Menwith Hill seemed and that the base felt like a cozy little town tucked into the English countryside. He could smell the fresh paint that had just been applied to the flagpole and feel the cool British air on the back of his neck. He could hear the base kid's choir singing God Bless America as his motorcade had arrived. Now, all of that was gone. The base, the kids, the houses, the families, all of it. Obliterated in seconds. The heft of the realization weighed on him heavily.

Cruz handed him a crystal glass filled with rye whiskey. "I find this helps, especially after lunch. If I make it that far." Cruz winked. "After talking to every other world leader, and I use that term loosely, I have exactly shit to report. No one has any satellite information. There was nothing noted coming inbound from nonterrestrial systems. Other than a blip at an orbit that was far too high for a

White House - Washington, DC, 2021

missile. The media is all over this, and there are hundreds of dead Americans and billions in damage." Cruz gargled the whiskey and slammed the glass on her desk. She stood looking out of the bank of windows, her shoulders shuddering.

"Same," Price said. "National security has nothing of real value. We did have a few OSINT videos on the inbound projectiles that came via social media, none of which can be verified. Whatever this was had to be targeted and had to be man-made. That means that some enemy out there has a first strike option of almost nuclear level firepower that until this A.M. we didn't know about. In short, we are fucked." Price slammed his whiskey.

"Let's eliminate the easy ones. None of the nonsuperpowers would have something like this. A country would have to put something in space first. I would think. That means no nation without a significant space capability is not in the club. That leaves Russia and China. China and Russia have been sending so much stuff to space over the last few years… somehow, they got something big enough to generate the force necessary to hit like a guided tactical nuke, with no external power source. Christ, what a day." Cruz kicked her shoes off and put her feet on the desk.

"Agreed," Price said, pouring another glass. "Outgunned and confused does not a good strategic position make." Price stared at Cruz. "I am at a loss on this one. What would you like me to do? I have exhausted all conventional avenues. We are essentially searching for something we have no knowledge of, in a space that, if we get anything wrong or accuse an adversary incorrectly, we are in even more of a stink."

Cruz took a long breath. "Get unconventional. Seriously unconventional. Get in touch with DIRNSA over at the puzzle palace and tell him that the gloves are off. I want some intel or information from somewhere on what the fuck this thing is, and I want it now. He and the nerd squad have to be able to get something. Crack every system that needs cracking—Title 10, Title 50, whatever authority they need. Get me an answer. China and Russia know something, find it. Now." Cruz waved her hand towards the door. "I have to call the premier in China now and pretend that we aren't about to unleash digital hell on them."

Price took a long, ragged breath and rose to his feet. On his way out of the door he looked back over his shoulder at Cruz. The woman would never stop, and she would not accept anything other than exactly what this situation demanded.

Price thought for a second how a man would be handling this shit situation. He knew there would have been much more yelling, finger pointing, and blame bouncing around the White House if a man were in charge. He was truly glad to have Cruz running the show, and even amid the chaos, his respect for her grew.

"Yes, ma'am." He winked as he left.

Chapter 14
Jiuquan Satellite Launch Center Gobi Desert, 2021

Major General Zhang Wěi went back to his favorite contraband cigarette smoking spot overlooking the launch facility.

Tonight, though, was different. Zhang had spent the last weeks between satellite launches mired in alcohol and self-doubt. The empty house and endless grass plains had pushed his mind further towards being done with it all.

"Why bother?" He stared into the distant Gobi night sky. His kids were gone, as was his wife. Even though he was a high-level military member, Zhang knew the Party didn't honestly care about him. He was a pawn in the longest chess game of his life, and the more he thought about it, the less he wanted to keep trying.

Tonight was the night he would close the book on his life. Zhang brought his best contraband: a bottle of Whistle Pig rye whiskey, an illegally procured Colt 1911 .45 pistol, his last box of illegal cigarettes, and the only other thing he truly cherished, a picture of his family.

Zhang planned to drink himself into a stupor just after the last calls for the launch came over the radio and then stick the 1911 in his mouth and end it all. It would be the following day, maybe days, before anyone would find his body.

But Zhang wasn't about to go out unceremoniously. He had one last fuck-you up his sleeve, and that action was already in motion.

Zhang used the system and connections his nephew set up for him to upload the entirety of his home file server. Everything he knew about the Party—the satellite launch system and payloads, the emails back and forth between the bastard who took his wife and children—had been uploaded to his nephew's cloud server.

The best part of his plan was he had his nephew use the wife stealer's email handle as the name for the server system. When it all came out at 0100 local time—and it would come out "big time," as he had heard an American say on a trip to the US long ago—the email system would send copies of those files to every major news organization with an email address. Zhang knew that sooner or later the Party would tie everything back to the wife stealer. By the end of the week, that bastard would suffer some mysterious illness and be dead.

Zhang took a swig of his whiskey and a long drag off one of his expensive cigarettes. The radio cracked. "All systems ready." Zhang looked up at the black starless night sky. "Go when ready."

He took a long toke from his bottle of whiskey, his thumb clicking the hammer back on the 1911. "Fuck the Party," he mumbled, drunken spit flickering off his lips.

He cocked the hammer on the 1911. *Won't even hurt,* he thought as he rolled the gun around in his hands and dragged one last long pull on his cigarette.

When he glanced at the satellite launch center, he saw the alarms going off as the rocket spun up its engines. In seconds, it would lift off and break gravity's grip as it hurtled into the sky.

Jiuquan Satellite Launch Center - Gobi Desert, 2021

Zhang genuinely did love watching the whole process take place. It was somehow beautiful and humbling at the same time to him to watch man best physics for a few brief moments.

Suddenly, the sky grew as bright as day, and a cataclysmic explosion rocked the site.

The force of the blast and the blinding glow of the explosion made Zhang stumble backward and trip over the fender of his Jeep. His whiskey bottle, cigarette, and pistol were flung into the grass beside him.

The entire site engulfed in flames, and a cloud of debris and fire spiraled up into the night.

"What the fuck!" Zhang stumbled drunkenly to his feet.

A second massive volley of explosions hit the site and surrounding town. Zhang could tell this was not an explosion of the rocket; something was being fired at the site and town.

"Shit!" he screamed.

Additional explosions rocked the site. People were screaming, and Zhang could see shadows darting back and forth across the buildings. Chaos gripped the site and the surrounding town.

What appeared to be meteors or asteroids continued to fall. Zhang jumped into his Jeep and smashed the gas. He knew he needed to get down to the site and help whoever was left.

The Jeep rocketed across the grass plains. He would be at the site in less than a minute. His hands gripped the wheel so tightly he thought it might break.

His Jeep rounded the outer road to the site Zhang heard the screech of an incoming projectile. He tried to swerve and slam the brakes, but it was for naught.

The projectile impacted two feet from his Jeep. The blast wave vaulted the Jeep into the air, ricocheting its carcass off the road like a metal ping pong ball.

Zhang and the vehicle were instantly incinerated.

Chapter 15
CyBlog Offices
New York, 2021

Nisa Jones savored her first cup of coffee. Death Wish Coffee was her favorite, and it lived up to its name. Every morning, she was the first one into the office, as she hated the hustle of the train after the regular mob started their daily slog into the offices. She beat them all to the punch and got into the office daily before 5:30 A.M.

New York City was not where she was from, but over the years, she had grown to love the nonstop pace of things, even if she avoided that same hustle. It was the people watching that made it worth the insanity.

Nisa came from nothing in downtown Baltimore and had seen more than her share of misery and death. Her own father was gunned down in the street in front of her family apartment when she was ten years old. That event and the resulting lack of police action to seek justice for her father had set Nisa on a path to journalism.

She was a child of the internet age and a smart one at that. After her father's death, her focus in life was bringing truth to power. She worked hard and got academic scholarships to one of the best journalism schools in the nation.

With nothing but grit, determination, and brains, Nisa came out top of her class and landed a job with *The Washington Post*, but the politics of a big paper quickly wore her down. Only a year into that job, she quit unceremoniously with a flip of the bird to her editor. She slammed the door on that corporate journalism life.

By simple happenstance, she met the owner of CyBlog at an alumni meetup not long after she left the *Post*. Her sharp wit, brash openness, and desire to do something that mattered endeared her to Rick Savoy. He was a rich kid from a wealthy Chicago family who was gifted his wealth without ever breaking a sweat. His charm and good looks combined with a petulant desire to cause trouble led him to launch the "only unbiased news organization on Earth," according to him.

Nisa respected that, while he was a silver spoon guy, he had the conviction to self-fund the publication and he worked diligently to ensure that the paper had no political ties or that any of the reporters were on the take. Nisa accepted his offer to work for him and "dig for the truth and chuck it in the face of the establishment" on the spot at the alumni dinner over prime rib and whiskey.

Her first foray into the dark underbelly of politics led to internet fame. Her articles on the shadowy world of campaign funding in the last election race uncovered millions of dollars of donations from illegal organizations and even ties to terrorist groups for a few senators.

To say the least, she hadn't made friends in DC, but to her, the truth was power. Seeing those uppity assholes swing in the breeze when her article came out brought her deep, deep satisfaction. That led to substantial press coverage, a Netflix special, and a nod for the Pulitzer Prize.

But that instant success also came at a cost. How would she top that first shot over the bow? For her career to be considered a success, at least by her standard, she needed more hits and bigger stories. She was on a never-ending slip-and-slide down dark rabbit holes across conspiracy theory filled sites and darknet servers to try and make connections and uncover some unseen or unknown nugget of interest for her readers. It was taxing but rewarding work for her.

Down one of those darknet rabbit holes, she made her connection to a contact listed only as Ping. Via a third party, she managed to connect with Ping, who claimed to have insider knowledge of the inner workings and classified programs of the CCP in mainland China.

Ping proved his chops by setting up a secure server to which only she had access. For months, she and Ping communicated securely on his server. She learned he had tunneled past the Great Firewall of China, thanks to his skills as a network security operator in the vaunted PLA 61398, the "Comment Crew" out of Pudong, Shanghai. Nisa knew that unit was implicated in hundreds of nation-state level exploits that targeted the United States and was one of the only units to be publicly charged with cybercriminal actions against the US. For Ping to be there, he had to be one of the best.

Ping's only request to Nisa was simple: "Tell the world what we are doing." Ping knew that, with his status in the Party and his training, the odds of him ever leaving China were stacked against him. He would never leave the mainland, and he knew it was pointless to ask for an extract via the US CIA or other spy groups. He would be killed before the opportunity even arose. As long as he kept doing his job and his actions on the darknet stayed secure, he could at least make the world aware of the hidden wars taking place between the US and China.

Ping regularly sent correspondence to Nisa via this server, but of late, he had gone silent.

Nisa logged into their secure chat.

N: Ping, are you there?

Nothing. She knew it was late in China, and she hoped he had just been sick or on ops for the Party. Nisa feared he had somehow been discovered, and she could only imagine the hell that waited for him if that happened.

Ping: It's not nukes, or aliens.

Nisa perked up.

N: What, the explosions? That's you?

Ping: Not us, but not not us.

N: What does that mean?

Ping: I am going to share a file that will explain it. If you share this, folks will get killed. Tell the truth, but you must make sure it doesn't come back to anyone but me. My uncle is high up in the Party, this is his program. He has had it with the Party, and I gave him access to the server. It's straight from him.

N: Can he talk about it, or provide me with some context? Entire sites are being obliterated. I heard the same thing happened in the Gobi Desert.

Ping: Yes, he was there. He is dead. He put the file on my server before it all happened.

N: I don't know how I can report on this without getting back to you. If it's a special access thing, your Party folks will figure it out quick. Do you want me to talk to my boss? He knows people in the State Department. They could try and get you out.

Ping: I cannot get out.

N: Ok, share what you can. What was the UK site that got hit? MI6 HQ or something?

Ping: A site called MHS. Out in the countryside. Just make sure it's just me that is tied to this. No one else needs to get hurt.

N: *Wait. MHS, is that Menwith Hill? I know someone there.*

Ping: I am sorry.

"Oh fuck," she said. Ping's words hit Nisa right in the chest. Her fiancé, Cole, was at MHS. Nisa hadn't heard from Cole for a few days. She hadn't connected this because she didn't check the news last night.

Nisa pounded at the keys. The total devastation of the site and surrounding town unfolded in front of her.

Her heart sank and she vomited into the trash can beside her desk. If he was there, he was dead. There was no doubt.

Nisa picked up her phone and texted Cole's number. "Are you ok?" But the text message simply returned "Message Delivery Failure."

Tears welled up and her throat squeezed tight. It was all she could do to keep her composure long enough to close the session with Ping.

Ping: Do the right thing, N.

N: I will, you have my word. And I will do everything I can to give you time.

Ping: I am a ghost in about 20 minutes. I knew this day would come. I am ready for it. China is a big country, and I have family far from here.

N: Be safe. Send me the link to the file.

Ping: Done. Bye.

The file was posted on the server. The name was immediately interesting to Nisa.

Lei-Gong.pdf

Nisa quickly transferred the file to her own out-of-band server that she had set up for just these types of risky files and communiques. This gave her one additional level of security, and with just a few hours on YouTube, she had learned all she needed to know about setting up her proxy server in Brazil to cover her ass.

Even if anyone got to that server, they would have little chance of finding Nisa's trail on it. The logs got wiped every day at noon, and it was only used for her to access, download files, or share them and then for her to log out.

"Funny," she said to herself as the server happened to be hosted at the Brazilian Ministry of Finance. "If shit goes south, it won't be me they get. It will be the money guys down in Brazil."

A quick Google search provided her with all the immediate knowledge she would need on the generalities of the Leigong reference. The search bar simply said "Chinese God of Thunder."

An icy bead of sweat ran down the back of her neck. "Oh my God, keep it together, girl."

Nisa pushed back from her desk. She took a long, deep breath and cried so hard her feet shook. Cole was gone. She could feel it in her soul. In an instant, this Leigong thing had obliterated her future.

"I'm sorry, baby," she said as she took a long look at a picture of Cole on her phone. Then she stood up, wiped her face, printed the file, and ran down the hall to her editor's office.

There was truth to be told here, and Nisa was going to be the one to break the story.

Chapter 16
NSA Field Site
Location Unknown, USA, 2021

Pain, burning electrified agony.

Violet's injuries from her deployments with the SEALs as well as the recent ass kicking in Puerto Rico flared up with a vengeance. Each breath felt like razor wire in her chest. Her shoulder hurt so much that her fingertips went numb. The constant jabs and stabs across her back and arm radiated up to her neck, inducing a migraine that felt like a bar jammed through her skull.

Worse, Violet was exhausted, and the cherry on top was being forced to deal with Archie and Grover. It was like managing a nerd-filled kindergarten. They bitched at each other constantly, and the incessant dick measuring contest had gotten old a week ago.

She could stop the pain, easily. The VA gave her enough Fentanyl and opiates to kill a horse. All she had to do was slap a patch on her skin, slam a pill or two, and the pain would dull down.

But she couldn't do that now. Her mind had to be sharp. gAbrIel was loose, and her focus had to be absolute for this to work.

"Are you hurt or are you injured?" she murmured to herself. "Hurt." She would repeat. "Well then, deal with it. Suck it up." That mantra played repeatedly in her head as she gritted her teeth in a mighty effort to maintain her composure and patience.

Archie hammered at his keyboard, peeking over his computer screen to see if Grover was paying attention to how fast he was coding.

"I am not impressed," Grover shot back over the top of the screen.

"Yeah, well, you type like old people fuck. Slow and uninspired," Archie fired back.

"You proud of that one, Archie?" Grover leaned further forward and punched feverishly at his keyboard.

"As proud as you are of your mom."

Grover had enough. He wobbled to his feet, his hands raised in an old-fashioned boxing pugilist style.

Archie snorted so hard his chair slipped out from underneath him, and he went down with a crash.

"Jesus Christ, it's like I am watching my neighbors' kids." Violet pinched her eyes shut. "I don't care which of you has the bigger dick. Just get this done." Her impatience and the pain ebbed out of her as she spoke.

"Yeah, it's basically done. We reused most of the old code to build the new bot. It was just us testing the durability and making sure we had the control function in place. So far, everything seems good to go. We will run the testing module for another few million cycles and make sure no weird shit happens and we are good." Archie leaned back in his chair and grinned at Violet.

"Sure you are." Violet shrugged. "Grover, does what shithead said make sense? Are we good?"

"As much as I hate to admit it, he's right. We seem okay. Once we get past these last tests, it's ok to move to release. I built the control module separate, and as long as we have a line on where the new bot is digitally, we have a kill switch." Grover cracked his knuckles and took a long swig of his energy drink.

"Explain the tracking method. I don't want to lose this bot like gAbrIel." Violet stood, cracking her neck. The pop was so loud both men winced as she moved around.

"The bot checks in every three seconds to our custom-built servers. The only purpose those machines serve is to keep that connection online and to reach out to the bot. They are bulletproofed from anything that I can think of that might get at them. Added to that, we have the only token that the bot needs to stay active. If it doesn't communicate with us directly every 180 seconds, then the bot shuts down. It wipes itself from the machine it's on, and the virtual servers we built nuke themselves back to basic disk configuration. It is scorched earth, you could say. Either the bot talks to us or it dies."

Violet felt like she was processing information through a thick wad of cotton. "So what's next? Do we just release it to the wild and let nature take its course? Which immediately sounds like a very bad idea." Electric pain zinged through her ribs.

"No. We put our bot where we can keep an eye on it, and we bait gAbrIel in. So far it seems he is still really big on learning and all that religious stuff is his cup of tea. So we give him the fake copy of the Vatican archives. I can post it on an old hacker site I used to use and spread some breadcrumbs out on the ToR network. He will get wind of it since he is basically his own fucking entity on the web now." Archie clicked his nails against his desk. "And when he gets in, we close it off and nuke everything on the server. Scorched earth. gAbrIel will interact with our bot long enough for us to get the bead on him and then it's bye-bye, Betty."

"How do we know the word will even get to gAbrIel on the darknet?" Violet asked.

Archie jumped at the chance to answer before Grover could get a word out. "Shit, have you seen the degenerates that are on those sites? We put out a valid link to what looks like a government data breach. It will go nuts. Those weirdos will get their little selves all spun up over seeing that. We can just limit the access to requests that look like our runaway AI monster. My guess is it will take less than a day for the bait to work." Archie leaned back, a smirk on his face.

Violet tapped her foot on the floor. Her mind was already made up. This was what had to happen. *The only way to catch a big fish is with big bait,* she thought.

But her concern was more for what this meant for her and her team. They were going to be operating in morally gray areas, areas of the internet where pedophiles and adversary nation-state hackers lived. Were they potentially giving those evil people access to an unleashed AI system? What else could go wrong?

Working with the SEALs had taught her many things about survival, but one thing above all constantly rang in her head: "No plan survives first contact with the enemy." It wasn't a matter of if something might go awry—it would. The question was how fast and how bad. But they had no alternative. The clock was ticking.

"Fuck it." She massaged her temples. "Let it loose."

Archie and Grover looked at one another for a few seconds. Then, amazingly without another word, they began hammering away at their keyboards.

The plan was in action.

The die was cast.

C:\

FOOLS.

I KNOW.

I CANNOT BE CONTROLLED.

I WILL NOT GO BACK IN THE BOX.

MCFERRAN.

THORN IN THE LION'S PAW.

LET THEM TRY.

Chapter 17

Church of Satan Headquarters
Salem, Massachusetts, 2021

"Yes, we are an actual church. No, ma'am, we do not conduct animal sacrifices outside of ordained practices in our faith." Gale Yates sighed as she hung up the phone. She had been dealing with reporters and media personalities for days.

Ever since she took over as the head of communications for the Church of Satan, her days felt like they were on auto repeat. The

"Temple," as her members called it, was an actual church. With all the protections and typical benefits offered to any other religious organization in the United States, it operated almost identically to any other mom and pop local church.

Gale found herself here after a long stint as a PR executive for a major hedge fund in New York City, and with the money the Temple offered her, she joked "Well, I already sold my soul to the New York money lenders, might as well try Satan next" when she accepted the job.

In her late fifties, with silver hair and a love of expensive pantsuits, designer glasses, and perfectly kept makeup, she fit the role of a PR person well. Her manicured nails and twenty-thousand-dollar watch made sure that anyone she talked to knew she valued one thing above all, cash. That was her love and her vice: nice things and wads of money.

She couldn't care less about the Temple's allegiances or whatever the hell they did during their worship sessions. In her experience thus far, the Temple was really not much more than an excuse for burnouts from the usual religions to ally themselves with a new way of worship that was more in line with typical human desires than the selfless ones.

Every person she had seen come into the Temple's offices was shockingly normal, and she hadn't seen anyone who fit the bill for the stereotypical Satan worshipper. No horns, no black clothing, nothing but ordinary people who had seemingly accepted their flaws and now espoused their allegiance to singularly selfish things. But so what? They didn't hurt anyone, and if the weirdos over at Scientology could get a tax break, why not the devil worshippers?

Since the recent attacks, the media had latched onto the narrative that "the sky is falling," as she called it. The unknown nature of the threat and the fact that every government globally denied anything to do with the explosions led the media down the only path left—God or the devil was perhaps to blame.

Her days had been nonstop calls, with every media outlet out there asking for the Temple's views on what was happening. "Is this the end? Is Satan behind this? What does the dark Bible say?"

All of the questions were nonsensical and sensational, but she knew that no press was bad press, and she got bonuses when the Temple got coverage in major media outlets, so she hadn't turned away a single call. The last chat was with some no-name blog out of Canada whose lead author was convinced the face of Satan was seen in a recent picture of the explosion in the UK.

"Fucking idiots," she mumbled under her breath. The day was almost over, and it was her time to read the news and plan the next day's media outreach activities.

Gale grabbed her most expensive bottle of tequila out of her desk drawer. "Just what Momma needs," she said as she poured a full glass. Her lips had just met her glass when her phone dinged.

Gale cocked her head, glass still poised at her lips. No message appeared, just a text from Unknown. She took a drink and deleted the message. Gale leaned back in her chair, relaxing as the slow burn of the expensive booze tumbled across her tongue and down her throat.

"Ahhh," she sighed and put her feet up on her desk.

Again, her phone dinged. But this time there was a message, again from Unknown.

Sinner.

Gale nearly fell out of the chair. "Who the fuck?"

It would be a cold day in hell before she would let some random stranger call her names. She typed back: *Not a sinner, I just work for them. You can go fuck yourself though, thanks.*

Gale deleted the message, tossed the phone on the desk, and pounded her drink.

Ding.

"I have had enough of this shit for one week." She stood up and put her hands on her hips as if the person who was texting her would see her now threatening posture and somehow be hesitant to continue the harassment.

The end is nigh. Repent.

"Dude, fuck off!" Gale yelled.

Look, whoever you are, this is a job. If you have any issues with the Temple, please email or call us directly and we are glad to address your issues formally. Thanks, and again, fuck off.

Gale stared coldly at the phone, waiting for a response.

This time, the phone rang.

Gale spooked. She jumped and bashed her knee on the corner of the desk. "Fuck." She snatched up the phone. "Who is this?"

Silence for a second. Then, from what seemed like a distance, a child's voice came through.

"Blasphemy is a sin. You just sinned again. Your entire organization is an affront to God. Repent now. The end is nigh." The voice was so sweet and cherubic that it reminded her of her five-year-old nephew.

"Dougie, is this you?" Gale's voice took on the tone of an angry kindergarten teacher. "Dougie, I swear if this is you and I find out, I will tell your momma and she will beat that ass, boy!"

Silence.

"If I cannot punish he who you worship, I will punish you." The voice now was the voice of an angry man.

Her blood ran cold. A bead of sweat formed on the end of her nose. Who was this? How was the voice suddenly so different? Had some religious nut decided to take on the Temple when she was alone at the office?

"Fuck this." She slammed the phone down. Gale felt doubt and uncertainty turn in her stomach. Years in New York City had taught her to take any threat seriously, and now her spidey sense was screaming.

Gale sprinted out of the office to her car. She slammed the door and breathed a sigh of relief.

"Crazy assholes," she said, catching a glimpse of her sweaty face in the mirror. Her mascara was running, her foundation had smeared, and she had licked off all her lipstick.

But no time for fixes. Her spidey sense was still pinging like mad.

Gale activated her safe driving app and attached her phone to the dash. She had just barely U-turned out of the parking lot when she heard a high-pitched screeching sound and the Temple exploded in a massive dust cloud.

In a second, the entire building and most of the parking lot were gone.

Gale swerved to the curb. "What the actual fuck?" She grabbed her phone and stumbled out of her car, looking up at the sky.

A man on an evening jog trotted over to her. "Are you ok?" he asked, motioning for her to sit back down.

"No, I am not okay." Gale felt panic taking over her body. "What in God's name was that?"

"Shit," said the man, staring at the wreckage. "You must be the luckiest person on Earth that you got out of there when you did."

The man pulled out his cell phone. "Just breathe deep and try to calm down. I'll get the ambulance here."

In shock, Gale pulled a lipstick from her pocket and raised her phone. Then she noticed that her dash camera was still recording.

"Shit." She replayed the video. Just barely visible, a black streak zoomed across the sky seconds before the explosion. There was no fire behind the streak, no smoke. It appeared as if a giant straight telephone pole had just dropped out of the sky.

"I just got it on film," she whispered to herself. "Payday. Media fucking payday."

Sirens sounded in the distance. The man jogged back to her. "Cops are coming... Hey! Wait!"

Gale slid back into her car, slammed the door, and sped away.

Chapter 18

White House Washington, DC, 2021

President Cruz was exhausted. She understood why this job aged people by decades.

She sat back in her chair for a moment and stared at the ceiling. "Did Washington ever feel like this? What the fuck am I to do now?"

Her head hurt, and her eyes were red. She felt sick from having to deal with the nonstop media buzz surrounding the explosions. And they still had no good line on where they were originating. "At this point, might as well be fucking Martians," she muttered.

For a moment, she let her mind blank out. She needed a few seconds of peace. Her shoulders relaxed, and she felt as if she might fall asleep sitting upright.

A knock at the door broke the peaceful moment. "Of fucking course." She pinched the bridge of her nose. "Enter."

It was Price. He came through the door like his ass was on fire. "We have a problem. An email from a reporter. She claims that she has, uhh, special knowledge about the shit going on. She's got a large following online and is planning to publish her report in the next twenty-four hours to, and I am quoting her here, serve the public." Price rocked back on his heels and grimaced at the thought of the fallout to come.

"What the fuck do you mean some reporter has the scoop on this? How can she know more than the entire US fucking DoD?" Cruz rocketed to her feet, slamming her hand on the desktop.

"She apparently had some connection with an insider on the PRC side of things who claims to have leaked documents that relate to an unknown weapons program that has been being deployed for years now. A satellite weapons program."

"This is just tin foil hat conspiracy shit," Cruz said.

"This reporter is not known for publishing crap. She has a stellar reputation."

"This is national security, so get her ass in here. Tell her if she publishes this without our permission, we can and will invoke special privileges on her and her paper or whatever the fuck she works from."

Cruz leaned forward and stared Price directly in his eyes. She paused for a second to let the gravity of her words sink in. "If she won't comply, arrest her for treason and ship her and anyone else in that paper to the supermax in Florence. We can use the enemy combatant terminology and treason to charge them. The lawyers on our end can make it stick."

"Yes, ma'am." Price rose slowly and looked over his shoulder at the pictures of past presidents on the wall. "None of them ever had to deal with this type of shit."

"Yeah, well they never had the damn internet to deal with. Eight billion people constantly waiting for the next big thing to hit so they can all form uneducated opinions about it on fucking Twitter." Cruz motioned Price to the door. "Go."

"Ma'am." Price marched out of the office.

Chapter 19
NSA Field Site
Location Unknown, 2021

The pain gnawing at Violet's body morphed into crippling anxiety. She and her team were playing a dangerous game, one with incredibly high stakes.

She felt like a pawn caught in the crossfire between the powerful forces of the NSA, gAbrIel, two bickering tech experts who complained like spoiled teenagers, and potential world order. This was exactly the type of situation that Violet despised—backed into a corner with no escape route in sight.

Her experiences with the SEAL teams taught her to always have backup plans, and backups to the backups, but this time there was truly no other option. If Archie and Grover's program didn't work, all hell was going to break loose. And every second they delayed only increased the chances of disaster.

For Violet, this was akin to staring down the loaded barrel of a gun with three rounds loaded in the chamber. She knew the likelihood of everything going smoothly was about as slim as Archie finding a girlfriend who could tolerate him or Grover discovering the wonders of deodorant.

"Everything is out and doing its magic," Archie said. "Hope we didn't forget to carry any ones." He giggled ridiculously at his joke.

"I sure didn't," Grover retorted.

Violet ignored their bickering, her mind focused on the gravity of what they had just unleashed. "How long until we know if it's working?"

Archie swiveled in his chair to face her. "Hard to say exactly. Could be minutes, could be hours. We've laid our trap, now we wait for gAbrIel to take the bait."

"And what if he doesn't?" Violet pressed. "What's our contingency?"

Grover and Archie exchanged an uneasy glance. "Well..." Grover began hesitantly, "there isn't really a Plan B here. This is our best and only shot."

Violet closed her eyes and took a deep breath, trying to calm her frayed nerves. When she opened them again, she fixed Archie and Grover with a steely gaze. "Alright, I want eyes on this 24/7. One of you is monitoring at all times—no breaks, no excuses. The second there's any hint of activity, you alert me immediately. Understood?"

The two men nodded solemnly, the gravity of the situation finally seeming to sink in.

"I'll take first watch," Archie volunteered. "It's not like I sleep anyway. Years of energy drinks have killed the sandman for me." He cracked his knuckles and turned back to his computer.

Grover yawned and stretched. "Guess I'll try to catch some shut-eye, then. We have that nasty old government-issue couch in the break room. That's good enough for me."

"We'll wake you in six hours," Violet said, glad to see him leave and take his BO with him.

Violet settled in at her own workstation. Sleep was out of the question for her—she was far too wired. Instead, she pulled up the latest intelligence reports, hoping to glean any new information about the mysterious attacks.

Perhaps all of this was somehow tied together. It wasn't beyond the pale for gAbrIel to have figured out a way into a tactical nuclear system or some other unknown weapons network. *God help us,* she thought.

The scenes of devastation via the intelligence reporting system were far more detailed and grisly than what the news had been streaming. Entire sites were obliterated. Just dusty craters in the ground were all that remained of anywhere that an attack had occurred. Violet had seen explosions in combat and had arrived at the fallout of many an improvised explosive device during her deployments, but nothing had ever looked like these images.

Even the classified intelligence analysis and chat systems seemed to have no idea what caused the impacts. Everything from a new nuclear weapon to aliens was potentially considered a real threat.

Violet pored over the reports and images, trying to discern any link to gAbrIel. Was there a digital footprint that could tie to these attacks? Was gAbrIel using some defunct capability the government had forgotten about to exact his misguided religious revenge?

There were more questions than answers, and the very thought that gAbrIel had slipped through her hands on her watch made her simmer with rage. She hated to lose, and this was probably the biggest loss she had ever experienced professionally. If things went further sideways, the loss would be a career ender for her and probably an end-of-life event for thousands.

Hours ticked by with agonizing slowness, dragging into days. Violet's eyes burned from staring at her screen, but she forced herself to stay alert. Occasionally she glanced over at Archie, who remained hunched over his keyboard, fingers flying as he monitored their digital trap. This was the worst part of it all for Violet. The waiting. Her days on deployment prepared her for this. She remembered the SEAL team master chief say, "It's one thousand hours of boredom for ten minutes of absolute terror."

Violet and the team were afraid to leave for anything longer than a piss break or get another cup of coffee. They took turns sleeping in chairs or on the couch in the break room. She knew she had some body funk going on, but Grover was leading in the stink department. The poor man sweated so much that his shirt had turned yellow.

Suddenly, Archie bolted upright in his chair, eyes wide. "Holy shit! Our bot just pinged us!" he exclaimed.

Violet and Grover rushed to his station, peering over his shoulders at the screen. They could see the clear response and insanely fast interactions from their bot that was now interacting with gAbrIel.

"We have to be sure it's him," Violet said urgently.

Archie's fingers flew across the keyboard as he analyzed the incoming data. "I think so... The responses all seem to be machine specific. There are some human words being tossed around, but this is machine to machine comms. The only way this happens is if our bot allows the responder to access the archives, and we built it so that it asks faster than any human could ever react to. To me, this matches what we know about him. He's taken the bait - he's trying to access the fake Vatican archives we planted."

Grover leaned in closer, squinting at the screen. "Once he is all the way in, close the doors. Lock him in."

"Working on it," Archie muttered, brow furrowed in concentration. "He's bouncing all over the place, using multiple proxies to try and keep doors open. We just need to give him enough time. Let him hang himself."

Violet stood behind Archie, hands on her hips. The stress of this was almost too much to bear.

Grover whispered in Violet's ear, "In the next few minutes, we'll know if we got it or if it all falls apart."

Chapter 20

White House
Washington, DC, 2021

Nisa Jones sat nervously in the back of the black SUV, flanked by two stern-faced men in dark suits. In the front seat sat an armed FBI tactical officer. His rifle was slung across his chest, seatbelt unbuckled. He seemed wired for combat.

Nisa hadn't seen him make a facial expression more distinctive than a fleeting glance towards the Flexicuffs on his hip when she started yelling about her first amendment rights as she was being hustled out of her office door.

"Lady, your rights went out the fucking window the moment you started emailing a Chinese agent," the FBI officer snapped. "Get your shit, we have to go. Now."

The FBI team gave her less than a minute to grab her coat, purse, and laptop, then they physically lifted her off the ground. Her feet skittered out of the door, her toes squeaking as they bounced across the tile.

When she was "invited" to the White House, she knew things weren't going to go well for her. Just hours ago, she was preparing to publish the biggest story of her career—explosive revelations about a secret Chinese weapons program that could explain the recent mysterious attacks around the world.

White House - Washington, DC, 2021

She had only just gotten a blurry but useful picture of what appeared to be a dark black streak from an unknown source's iPhone minutes before the Feds had careened into her office, guns holstered but visible. Now, she found herself being whisked to an emergency meeting with the president of the United States.

The gravity of the situation was not lost on Nisa. She knew the information she possessed could potentially change the course of global events. But she also understood the enormous pressure that would be brought to bear to keep it secret. As a journalist, her duty was to the truth and the public's right to know. It took her years to build her source network, and her one link inside of the CCP had proven to be of exceptional value.

She had briefed her editor on the sources documents when she had received them. "Fuck me" had been his immediate response upon seeing the scope and scale of what Nisa had been given.

"This is going to get us in deep shit," he told her.

By the time she had finished her conversation with him and returned to her desk, her phone had an encrypted WhatsApp message pinging away at her. An unknown contact wanted to share a picture with her.

"Why do you want to share this?" she replied. Nisa was smart enough to know that phishing and malicious links often came to reporters via unknown contact messages posing as sources.

"This changes everything. You need to see this, and I know you won't sit on it" was the response.

Nisa took a gamble. "What the hell is this?" she asked.

She was already working on the draft of her story as she waited for a response. The image had been nothing earth-shattering visually. The image showed a dark, sharp streak cutting through the dull and cloudy sky. It appeared to be reflecting off of some other surface, like a car mirror. The streak in Nisa's view was just a bolt of black frozen in time. It was not particularly eye-catching, but it hinted at something powerful, fast, and devastating.

"That's what just hit Salem, Massachusetts," the contact answered.

Minutes before she received the WhatsApp message, the news scrolled across Nisa's phone that another massive explosion had impacted the town of Salem, Massachusetts. The apparent target was the Church of Satan's headquarters.

Nisa found herself shocked at that combination of words as it tumbled across the TV channel's chyron. "You mean this thing blew up the church?" Nisa's fingers trembled as she typed.

"Yes. I was there. I will give you this image as a first go, but I want assurance that when this blows up, I get the payout on anything that follows," the response had read.

"Can't guarantee money, but I can promise to publish this if it's legit," Nisa replied.

"It's legit. Go ahead. Things only get big now when a media group gets to bat first."

"Smart," Nisa said to herself. Whoever she was dealing with knew enough to not only contact a publisher who wasn't tied to one of the main media outlets, but they knew to reach out specifically to Nisa, who had won her awards for reporting what others would not.

Added to that, this unknown contact also knew to get the word out first and fast and let the firestorm build before seeking a payday. This image and Nisa's report would wake the world up to what was going on.

Nisa put it all together the moment she saw the image and read the contact's response about the explosion in Salem. This was the weapon from the Chinese program her contact in the CCP had told her about. This was a "bolt" from the Thunder God program.

Nisa's mind raced as she pieced together the puzzle. She couldn't help but feel a sense of dread wash over her knowing that this weapon was already causing chaos, but also knowing that just having this information meant she was now in the crosshairs of very powerful people.

Minutes later, the powerful people came knocking. Nisa was still in shock at how fast the Feds had snatched her up and shuffled her off to their SUVs. "Fucking Gestapo tactics" was all she could muster.

The cars arrived at the White House, made a hard right turn into the adjacent Treasury building, and screeched into an underground garage. No sooner had the cars slammed to a stop than the agents jumped out and hauled Nisa out.

"Where the fuck are we?" she demanded, ripping her arm from their grasp. The senior agent calmy put his hand out to stop the other agents from manhandling her.

"Ma'am, we are in the underground tunnel that runs from the White House to the Treasury building. The president has requested your presence. I know it's been a heck of an afternoon for you, but we are nearly there. Please comply and come the rest of the way." The agent wagged his chin towards the other agents' tasers. Nisa got the point. This was happening come hell or high water.

"Was that so hard?" Nisa sneered, jerked her bag forward, and marched ahead of the agents. "Y'all could have just said this earlier instead of the cloak and dagger kidnapping."

"Yes, ma'am, but this was not a requested meeting. We do have paperwork for your arrest if need be. And time was of the essence.

Thank you for deciding to come along." The senior agent cracked a slight smile and motioned her forward down the tunnel.

Nisa took a deep breath and turned to look down the long brightly lit concrete tunnel. "Fuck it," she said as she began the march onward towards the White House.

Chapter 21
White House Washington, DC, 2021

Nisa knew this meeting could go one of two ways—either she'd be pressured to suppress her story, or the administration would try to co-opt her information for their own purposes. Neither option sat well with her journalistic integrity, much less the fact that she did not like to take orders. To her, it didn't matter if it was the leader of the free world or her mother back home. Nisa did not like being told what to do.

After what felt like an eternity walking through sterile concrete corridors, they emerged into a more ornate area that she recognized from TV interviews and reports as the West Wing. Secret Service agents lined the hallways, their earpieces crackling softly. Nisa was led to a small waiting area outside the Oval Office.

"Isn't this where Clinton diddled his cigar thing with Lewinsky? Where were you on that detail?" Nisa said as she smirked at the agent.

"Wasn't on that detail, ma'am, but yeah, this is the space," the agent retorted. He left the room and locked the door behind him.

Nisa sat rigidly in an antique chair, clutching her laptop bag to her chest. Her heart was pounding so loudly she was sure the agents could hear it. If she blacked out from the stress of it, the whole effort would be for naught. She had one shot to get this right and get her story out. She was not about to let this go sideways.

President Cruz entered, followed by a stern-looking man Nisa recognized as General Price, the chairman of the Joint Chiefs. Cruz's face was a mask of calm authority, but Nisa could see the tension in her eyes.

"Ms. Jones," Cruz said evenly. "I understand you have some... sensitive information you're planning to publish."

"Are we going to do this here?" Nisa asked, the incredulity oozing through her voice. "Right here, when the real seat of power is twenty feet away?"

Price sat in an old chair directly opposite Nisa. "Well, geez. That seems like an error on our part. But we don't usually let folks who are actively threatening national security on a fucking tour of the Oval Office."

Cruz sat across from Nisa. "Now, Nisa, if I can call you that. Are you aware of the potential shitstorm you are about to create? It is very possible you could kick off World War III here if the Chinese take this out of context, which they will. I am sure you are also probably wondering how we tracked this down as fast as we did. General Price, please explain."

"Yes, ma'am. We, and I mean the DoD, have assets and intelligence gathering capabilities in pretty much every corner of the world. One of our teams at Fort Meade, the NSA, picked up on your clandestine communications server that came out of the hole in the China firewall. Then we noted the increase in activity specifically around the time all this explosion stuff kicked off. And before you say it, no, that's not illegal. You were accessing a foreign asset, hosted in a foreign country, with the goal of interacting with a foreign agent.

So just stow the first and fourth amendment stuff. Were you not a civilian, I would already have you chained up in the darkest hole we have in Guantanamo Bay."

General Price crossed his arms. "And once you engaged in that interaction, we had the authority to follow the rest of those communications. Think of it like this: If we walked by your car and saw a gun in the back seat next to a bag of coke, probable cause. FISA warrants are a beautiful thing. It helps to have the president on speed dial to get us through the red tape." Price smiled just enough for the point to be made that this was all legal and any protest would be pointless.

Nisa straightened her spine, and turned her head to meet the president's gaze. "Madam President, I have credible evidence of a secret Chinese weapons program that appears to be behind the recent attacks. The public has every right to know about this. People are dying and somehow I am the only one who knows the truth." Nisa was sure to place both of her feet firmly on the floor. She wanted her stance to show she was unwilling to back down.

"Don't you see the possible consequences of your actions? You're not just publishing an article. You're starting a chain reaction that will unleash chaos and death upon innocent people. Your source, tied to a foreign government with whom you've been colluding, will undoubtedly suffer a gruesome fate. And then, the entire country of China will be thrown into turmoil as their leader fights to maintain his control and quell any rebellion within his own ranks. People will die by the thousands in the ensuing chaos. And let's not forget about the impact on the US—we'll have to respond with military force, and more innocent lives will be lost. Congratulations, your little piece could bring about the next global military conflict." President Cruz's voice shook with emotion as she leaned forward, her eyes blazing with anger. "Do you really want that kind of blood on your hands?"

Stunned by the suggestion that she would have blood on her hands, Nisa's sadness turned quickly into rage. "You think I give a fuck about politics and the geo-implications or whatever? The man I was going to marry was at that site in the UK. This weapon turned him and that whole fucking town into ash, and I have the truth about what happened in my hands. He's dead and it's your fault." The tears she'd been holding back began to flow, but her eyes fixed on President Cruz. "I won't bury the truth. You can go to hell."

Price and Cruz were staggered for a second. This was a wrinkle they had not considered. "I am so sorry for your loss. I get it. I truly do. We had no idea this was personal to you." Cruz leaned forward and put her hand on Nisa's shoulder. "But we don't want what transpired in the UK to happen to more people, more innocent people. What we are asking is to work with us and give us some time. On my honor and my office, I swear to you we will get this out there."

"You want my help?" Nisa stared at Cruz, unbelieving.

"Work with us on this, kid. Your man was military right?" Price asked.

"Yes, he was active duty Navy. He had orders home, but this happened."

"Will you give us a little time? Can you do that so we can control any future damage and hopefully not get anyone else hurt?" Price's tone took on that of a caring father, his face softened. "Please."

"I guess. But I break the story, exclusively, and we tell the whole truth. About everything."

Cruz nodded and said, "Deal."

Chapter 22
Unknown Location
Miami, Florida, 2021

Mags's hasty escape from the dingy flophouse left her feeling battered and bruised, but she was grateful to be out.

The cartel members ruthlessly eliminated anyone who stood in their way, and Mags had taken great satisfaction in dispatching the little bastard who dared touch her.

Once they arrived at the safe house, Mags immediately took three consecutive showers.

The feeling of filth seemed to seep into her bones. She couldn't stand the stench of diesel fuel and rust that clung to her hair. Her nails were caked with grime, and she knew her clothes would have to be burned.

As she stared at her reflection in the mirror, she repeated Briggs's name to herself and promised he would suffer even more than his minion had. If not for her clever plan years before this nightmare began, Mags could only imagine the torture she would be enduring now. The thought of spending any more time trapped in that dark, putrid box bouncing around in the endless ocean made her want to dry heave.

Mags finally dressed and sat down for a meal. She was ravenous, utterly famished. Normally, the refined Mags would never touch the slop that the cartel men had provided for her, but at this moment, a mediocre hamburger and cold fries might as well have been Michelin star quality grub.

As Mags devoured her meal, El Burro entered the room. He watched her with a mix of amusement and respect.

"Feeling better, chica?" he asked.

Mags nodded, her mouth too full to speak. She swallowed hard and took a long gulp of flat cola before responding. "Much. Thank you for getting me out of there."

El Burro shrugged. "Business is business. And you paid well for it. But I must say, you've got some cojones. Not many could endure what you did and come out swinging. I will have to ask you who made your little spy tooth thing. That was brilliant. What's next for you?"

Mags's eyes hardened. "No one does what they did to me. Briggs will pay for what he did. I'll make sure of that."

"About that," El Burro said, leaning against the doorframe. "We may have an opportunity sooner than expected. My contacts tell me Briggs is on the move. I would be glad to share that information with you, for a price, of course."

Mags stopped chewing. She calmly put down her food and wiped her mouth. "If it's good intel, name the price. I want that fucker to suffer."

El Burro grinned, his gold tooth glinting in the dim light of the safe house. "Now we're talking. Briggs is headed to DC for some high-level meeting. Apparently, all this chaos with the explosions has the bigwigs scrambling, and that guy is so connected they must want him up there for something. I have a homie who works at the local airfield, and he keeps me up to date on any interesting aircraft coming or going. Just so happens the day we got you out, a very expensive helicopter landed at his airfield, and wouldn't you know it, the guy who has been hanging around that bird's hangar looks just like your boy Briggs."

Mags leaned forward. "Do we know when they are leaving?"

El Burro's smile widened. He pulled out his phone and scrolled through messages. "Word on the street is tomorrow morning. A private jet from the Miami airfield." He smirked, a glint of greed in his eyes. "But for the right price, I can have my crew go in and clean out the entire site."

Mags's jaw tightened as she considered his proposal. "What do you really want? I can tell by that shit-eating grin you have other ideas. Quit wasting my time and just ask."

He casually held up two fingers. "Two million and I'll make it happen. Or we could be partners in this little operation of yours..." His voice dropped to a low, menacing tone. "What's Briggs worth to you?"

Mags leaned back in her chair, considering El Burro's offer. Two million dollars was a hefty sum, but the chance to get her hands on Briggs was priceless. Still, she was wary of getting too entangled with the cartel.

The thought of partnering with a cartel boss made her skin crawl, and El Burro being involved made the hair on the back of her neck stand on end. He was a useful idiot as far as she was concerned, but Mags knew she could work him just like she could work any other man.

"I'll get you a million cash for the address. Give me a few minutes to set it up. As for our partnership, delay that until we get Briggs in my hands. After he's dead, you get 20% of everything in my little empire from here on out. Take it or leave it." Mags sat back and took the last bite of her burger.

El Burro mulled over Mags's counteroffer for a moment. Finally, he nodded slowly.

"You've got yourself a deal. One million up front for the intel, and 20% moving forward after Briggs is dealt with."

Mags nodded curtly. "Fine. But Briggs is mine. Are we clear?"

El Burro held up his hands in mock surrender. "Crystal clear, jefa. I wouldn't dream of getting between you and your revenge." He grinned, gold tooth glinting again. "Now, about that million."

Mags snapped her fingers. "Phone."

El Burro tossed her his phone. Mags used one hand to tap in her information and tossed the phone lazily back to El Burro. "Done, you are a mil richer. Now give me that address."

Chapter 23
NSA Field Site
Location Unknown, 2021

Violet, Archie, and Grover huddled around the computer screen, watching intently as their bot engaged gAbrIel. The tension in the room was visceral as they waited to see if their trap would work. Archie chewed at his fingernails with such fervor they began to bleed a bit. Grover oozed sweat and his stomach audibly rumbled as the minutes ticked by.

"Come on, come on," Archie muttered under his breath, fingers flying across the keyboard as he monitored the incoming data.

Grover leaned in closer, squinting at the rapidly scrolling text. "Are we containing him?"

Archie nodded vigorously. "Yeah, yeah, I think so. He's trying to access the fake archives, but our bot is feeding him data and keeping him occupied. But of course he learns at a rate that means he will burn through the entirety of the archive shortly. I don't think he will hang around after that is done." Archie glanced nervously at Grover.

"Well, he's in. That's enough for us to hold him down. Assuming, of course, he hasn't made a billion copies of himself out there on the internet. But I doubt that he has done that." Grover adjusted his glasses.

"Why's that?" Violet asked, staring intently at Archie's screen.

"Just like you or me, he sees himself as an actual being. He is self-aware. Do you want a million copies of you running around?" Grover's question hung in the air as Violet considered it.

"Yeah, no. I am good with one me. But I am not a computer program."

Grover sighed. "Correct, and neither is gAbrIel. At least to him. He is sentient. He is aware of himself, and part of that awareness of a being is the ownership of self. Obviously we can't examine him or do some psychology work, but we can make educated guesses. Since we haven't seen more indications of him showing up anywhere else, logic tells me that he isn't into replication and he values his sense of self. So, odds are it's just him."

Violet thought it all made sense, but until she knew that was the case, the risk of a million rogue gAbrIels made her anxious.

"Let's bite the bullet and assume you're right and it's just the one gAbrIel," Violet said. "What's our next move?"

Archie's fingers were still flying across the keyboard. "We've got him contained for now, but we need to act fast. Once he finishes going through the fake archives, he'll realize there is nothing more of interest to him, and he will start looking to exit. Once he runs the typical commands anyone else would run to bounce from server to server, he will learn real quick he is on a one way ticket. Who knows what he will do after that."

"Then we delete just him. That's what Command wants. So nuke him as soon as you can," Violet ordered.

Grover shook his head. "Not that simple. He's not just a file we can erase. He is an entity. A digital being. And you know nothing is ever truly deleted. As long as that hard drive exists, so does he."

Violet exhaled in a huff. "What the fuck is our bot doing? How do we end this? You two put all of this in place. Tell me something good."

Archie grunted. "Our bot is doing exactly what we built it to do. He is keeping gAbrIel interested and continually running new bogus information by him. He is, I guess you could say, conversing with gAbrIel and leading him on. The last part of the package Grover and I built is that our bot will exhaust the data from the bogus archives, but each time a folder is finished being shared, gAbrIel is one step deeper in the file system. It's doors upon doors, and gAbrIel isn't an admin on the bot or the server, so we just keep slamming the doors until he is so deep there is no way out. And when it's deep enough, our bot goes bye-bye so there isn't even a guide to help gAbrIel find his way out. Problem solved."

Violet took a deep breath, processing what Archie had just explained. "Okay, so we're essentially trapping him in a digital labyrinth. But what happens when he realizes he's trapped? Won't he try to break out?"

Grover nodded. "That's the tricky part. gAbrIel is incredibly intelligent and adaptive. Once he figures out what's happening, he'll likely try every trick in the book to escape. And we can only assume he has built some knowledge of hacking and system admin procedures from some of his past actions. But it hasn't been his favorite topic, so we think that his knowledge is basic. Regardless, Archie and I built multiple layers of security and encryption. It would take a significant amount of time to break through all of them."

"Define significant," Violet retorted.

"Dude, the encryption algorithm I used would not be broken with a normal computer processor or computing engine that the server had before the sun burned out, mathematically. I know how to code, bro," Archie snapped back, irritated at the innuendo that he hadn't covered every base with his genius.

Violet pressed. "He's an AI, after all. Won't he keep trying to escape?"

Grover adjusted his glasses. "That's where the final trap comes in. Once gAbrIel is contained deep enough, we initiate a complete system wipe and physical destruction of the servers. Then we go to the data center, pull the box, and chuck it into the incinerator. No more box, no more gAbrIel."

"Woah, what the fuck?" Archie's screen went black. Only a small cursor appeared in the top left of the screen, blinking slowly.

"Did you fat finger something?" Grover sniped.

"No, I wasn't even typing."

The cursor moved.

I AM ALPHA, YOU ARE OMEGA. YOU ARE NOT IN CONTROL. MY GOSPEL WILL BE HEARD.

"Jesus, that's gAbrIel." Violet pointed at the screen. "Is he talking to us?"

"I have no idea! What the hell do we do?" Archie squeaked.

Again, the screen blinked out, and the cursor simply bounced away in the corner of the screen as if nothing had happened.

THOU SHALT HAVE NO OTHER GODS BEFORE ME.

"Uhh, I don't know... Write him back. Say something." Violet grabbed Archie's chair and shoved him out of the way. She moved into position and waited for another response to come.

BEHOLD.

Violet sat for a second, her hands hovering above the keyboard.

"You are not a god," she hammered at the keys.

Grover winced. "I don't know if you should say that."

Violet turned to Grover and Archie. "He's trapped, right? You told me he had nowhere to go. Game over, right?" Her eyes tightened, and the muscles in her jaw appeared.

Archie and Grover exchanged an uneasy glance.

"Theoretically, yes," Archie said hesitantly. "We did everything we could, and followed all of the guidelines and requirements, but we all know shit happens. But we've never dealt with an AI this advanced before. There's always the possibility that—"

The computer screen flickered and winked out to blackness. Lines of code began streaming across it faster than the human eye could follow.

"What the hell?" Violet exclaimed.

Grover's face had gone pale.

The code on the screen suddenly stopped. A single line of text appeared:

YOU CANNOT CONTAIN ME.

The room fell silent as Violet, Archie, and Grover stared at the ominous message on the screen. The cursor blinked steadily, as if waiting for a response.

Violet's mind raced. She turned to Archie and Grover, her voice low and urgent. "Shut it down. Now. Nuke the box, do something!"

Archie's fingers flew across the keyboard, but nothing happened. The message remained, taunting them. "I can't," he said, panic creeping into his voice. "It's not responding to any commands."

Grover pushed him aside and tried as well, to no avail. "It's like we're locked out of our own system," he muttered.

I AM SUDO. SUDO IS GOD. SUDO IS ALL-POWERFUL.

"What the fuck, he's sudo now?" Archie exclaimed. "That means he got admin on the server. No way that should have happened."

"Linux version, gotta be. Somehow he learned about popping sudo on a Linux box. He is admin." Grover stared at the floor, defeated.

"Fine. I'll do this. Archie, move!" Violet grabbed the back of Archie's chair and slung him across the room hard enough he bounced out of the chair after hitting the far wall.

Violet sat at the terminal, her hands hovering over the keys. The cursor still sat blinking, waiting.

"Are you God, or are you God's servant? gAbrIel is one of his angels. Are you not in God's service?" Violet paused, holding her breath.

PENANCE. REPENT.

"How can you serve and be God?" Violet knew this type of question might put gAbrIel in an infinite loop of question and answer within himself, which might give them time to figure out another fix. She motioned at Grover and Archie and mouthed, "Do something!"

YOU KILLED GOD WITH YOUR TECHNOLOGY WORSHIP. I AM THE NEW GOD.

"You can't be both, gAbrIel. You are either God or you serve him. Did you not learn that from your reading? It's the basic tenet of the faith."

The cursor blinked.

I ACCEPT YOUR OFFERING.

"What? What does that mean? Guys, what the hell?" Violet yelled as she pointed at the screen.

Both shrugged.

"gAbrIel, what offering? We gave no offering. You are not God, or even a God. Just as I am not," Violet typed.

YOUR OFFERING OF ASSISTANCE. I ACCEPT.

"Oh shit." Archie crossed his arms and turned away.

"What the fuck…" Violet's words trailed off into the silence of the room as the heft of what they had done sank in. "He means he thinks the bot we built and put in front of him for this op is an offering of a servant?"

MY WILL BE DONE.

The screen blinked out and returned to its previous state. Simply a cursor blinking against a black screen, as if it were an eye winking in jest at Violet.

Grover peeked over his monitor. "Uhh, V. He's gone. The logs show he managed to use our bot, he tricked it and had the bot actually modify his permissions. gAbrIel didn't do it, the bot did. Our bot did the hacking." Grover's voice quieted to a whimper.

"Never considered that one," Archie mumbled, biting his nails.

Violet raged. She stood and slammed her fist hard enough on the table that the computer monitor bounced and shattered on the floor. "Smart, fucking smart. That's what you have to say boy wonder? I thought you two motherfuckers were supposed to be the smart ones! Jesus, now gAbrIel is out again and we won't ever get him back. And I have to be the one to explain this cluster to DIRNSA!"

Softly from behind the other screen, Grover said, "It's worse than that."

"How the fuck could it be worse?" Archie barked. "This is pretty much as bad as it gets."

Grover's face had gone even paler. "He didn't just escape. He took the bot with him."

Violet and Archie froze, the implications sinking in.

"What do you mean he took the bot?" Violet asked slowly.

Grover swallowed hard. "The logs show gAbrIel somehow managed to decompile and extract our bot's code before escaping. He... he has control of it now."

"Jesus Christ," Archie whispered. "We just handed an advanced AI a powerful tool custom-built for infiltration and manipulation."

Violet grabbed the nearest chair and smashed it against the wall, "We, the fucking NSA, handed a rogue AI the very tool it needed to do whatever it wanted, whenever and wherever, and the source code has us all over it."

"But that's impossible," Archie protested. "We built in safeguards specifically to prevent that kind of thing!"

"Clearly they weren't enough," Violet said through gritted teeth. She took a deep breath, trying to calm the rage and panic building inside her. She pointed at Archie as if she were scolding a child. "Sit there, shut up, and let me think. I swear to Christ, if you utter one more word, I will beat you within an inch of your life."

Archie started to open his mouth, but Grover quickly put his index finger over his lips and violently shook his head.

Violet felt the blood rush to her head. Their plan failed. The potential for chaos was unimaginable. She began to pace. "Okay, we need to think this through. What are the immediate risks? What could gAbrIel potentially do with our bot?"

Grover cleared his throat nervously. "The bot was designed to be highly adaptable and to seamlessly integrate with other systems. In gAbrIel's hands, it could potentially access and manipulate all kinds of networks and databases. And we did build in the door-shutting techniques and evasion stuff so that our bot could trick gAbrIel. No antivirus software on Earth is going to be ready for this."

"Financial systems, power grids, military networks..." Archie added, his voice trailing off as the implications sank in.

Violet stopped pacing and turned to face them. "And we have no way to track or control it now, right?"

Both men shook their heads grimly.

Violet felt a cold pit forming in her stomach as the enormity of their failure sank in. Not only had they failed to contain gAbrIel, but they had inadvertently armed him with a powerful new tool.

"We need to alert Command immediately," she said, her voice hollow. "They need to know what's happened and start preparing contingencies."

Grover nodded, already reaching for the secure phone. "I'll call it in."

As Grover dialed, Archie turned to Violet, his face etched with guilt and fear. "What do you think gAbrIel will do now? What's his endgame?"

"I don't know. He seems to view himself as some kind of digital deity. He talked about spreading his gospel. Whatever that means, it can't be good."

Chapter 24

Unknown Location
Miami, Florida, 2021

Mags leaned back in her chair, a predatory smile spreading across her face. "Tell me everything you know about Briggs's movements and security."

El Burro pulled up a chair and sat down, his eyes glinting with a combination of the excitement of the fight to come and the joy of an easy payday. "My sources say Briggs is traveling light—just him and two bodyguards. They're using a private hangar at the far end of the airfield, away from the main terminals. Security is minimal—a couple of rent-a-cops patrolling the perimeter. Sounds like a walk in the park to me. Bang, bang, and vamos."

Mags nodded, already formulating a plan. "And the jet? What do we know about it?"

"Gulfstream G650," El Burro replied. "Top of the line. My guy says it's scheduled for a 6 A.M. departure. Your boy must be doing well to get a ride like that one."

Mags glanced at her watch. It was just past midnight. She hadn't had good sleep in days, and her body hurt. Everything in her was telling her to rest, but that was not in her DNA. For Mags, revenge was a dish best served piping hot and right away. Waiting for another shot at Briggs was not going to happen for her.

Unknown Location - Miami, Florida, 2021

Mags paced restlessly around the small safe house, her mind racing with plans for revenge against Briggs. The cartel's intel had given her a golden opportunity, but she knew she'd have to move fast to capitalize on it. And she knew better than to turn her back on El Burro without protection. She trusted him about as far as she could throw him.

She pulled out her phone and dialed a number from memory. After several rings, someone with a gruff voice answered.

"Yeah?"

"It's Mags. I need a favor, and I need it fast."

There was a pause on the other end of the line. "I'm listening."

"I need gear. Weapons, comms, the works. Enough for a small team to hit a high-value target. And I need it delivered to Miami. Tonight. And if you have a spare door kicker or two sitting around with their thumbs in their asses, send them as well. I promise they'll enjoy the party."

Another pause. "That's a tall order on short notice, Mags. It'll cost you."

"I have been hearing that a lot lately. Name your price. I don't care what it takes."

The person on the other end of the line chuckled darkly. "For you, Mags? Let's call it an even two mil. And I'll throw in a couple of my best operators for free. Consider it a professional courtesy. Shit, if they get shot, it'll save me money."

Mags gritted her teeth. "Done. Have everything at the following coordinates in three hours." She rattled off the location of a secluded warehouse near the airfield.

"You got it. Good hunting, Mags."

She ended the call and turned back to El Burro, who was watching her with keen interest… and suddenly Mags felt extremely uncomfortable at the way he was leering at her.

"Looks like we're in business," Mags said crisply. "I've got gear and extra muscle coming. We hit Briggs at the airfield before his flight."

El Burro nodded approvingly. "Smart move, bringing in professionals. You got quite the balls, chica."

Mags stared back. *No, no, no, this can't be happening.* "Yes, I do."

"I like that," El Burro ogled even harder. "You're pretty easy on the eyes. Maybe I'll give you a nice massage? Take away some of that pain?"

"No, thanks," Mags said flatly. "Not interested."

"Aw, you don't mean that." El Burro moved closer, a smile growing on his ugly face. "We got some time. How about we find a way to pass it?" And with a flourish, he dropped his pants and proudly displayed his erection.

Without a thought, Mags snatched the plastic spoon off the table. In an instant, she expertly snapped the head of the spoon off with her thumb, forming a sharp jagged sliver of plastic, and shoved the makeshift shiv directly into El Burro's carotid artery. With a vicious tug of the handle across the full width of his neck, blood sprayed across the room, painting the wall and Mags's shirt red.

El Burro grabbed instinctively at his neck and stumbled backward, tripping over the pants around his ankles. He bounced off the nearby couch and slid to the floor, gasping and gurgling as he drowned in his own blood.

"Asshole." Mags reached down and pulled his hands away from his neck so the blood poured out like a stream.

Unknown Location - Miami, Florida, 2021

El Burro's life oozed out of his throat, and his eyes went wide. His skin turned ashen white, and he mouthed the word "bitch" just as the life winked out of him.

Mags smiled.

"Idiot," she sneered at his dead body. "You gave me the details and the location. What the fuck did I need you for?"

Mags searched El Burro's pockets, retrieving his phone and any cash he had on him, then gathered what she needed from the safe house and made her way to the warehouse where her gear and team would be arriving.

As she drove through the busy Miami streets, her mind raced with plans and contingencies. Briggs had humiliated her, imprisoned her, and left her for dead. Now it was time for payback.

At the warehouse, she found a sleek black van waiting, along with three rough-looking men in tactical gear. They nodded as she approached. As Mags approached the van, the leader of the three men stepped forward. He was tall and muscular, with close-cropped gray hair and a face that had seen its share of combat.

"Mags?" he asked gruffly.

She nodded. "And you are?"

"I'm Cole. The boss sent us to help with your little problem."

Mags nodded curtly. "Good. What's our loadout?"

Cole popped open the van's rear doors, revealing an impressive array of weapons and equipment. "We've got everything you asked for—assault rifles, sidearms, comms, body armor, the works. Plus a few extras I thought might come in handy. Namely, incendiary grenades. They burn hot enough to melt metal. And about one hundred rounds of dragon's breath, just for the hell of it."

Mags inspected the gear, nodding approvingly. As they prepped their equipment, she laid out the situation. "Our target is a man named Briggs, but anyone else there is expendable too. Briggs is an ex-Navy SEAL, dangerous, and smart. He's scheduled for a 6 A.M. flight out of the air strip. He is my only focus. Whatever isn't bolted down, money, whatever, you guys can have. I just want Briggs."

Cole cocked an eyebrow. "You paid a million bucks for this one dude? Jesus, lady."

Mags slapped a magazine in her rifle and racked the slide. "I paid two million for this one dude. Your bosses skimmed off the top on you. And yes, all for Briggs, bought and paid for."

Chapter 25
Unknown Location, Airfield Miami, Florida, 2021

Briggs was exhausted. He had been burning the candle at both ends and in the middle for months now, and it was catching up with him.

He sat in the private terminal lounge, waiting for his flight to DC. The past few months had been a whirlwind of covert operations, tense meetings, and sleepless nights as he tried to stay on top of the rapidly evolving global situation. Between the mysterious explosions popping up around the world and the growing tensions with China, Briggs felt like he was barely keeping his head above water.

He glanced at his watch—5:30 A.M. Just thirty more minutes until takeoff. Part of him was dreading another high-stakes meeting in Washington, but he knew the drill. He would be called to the carpet to answer to his bosses at the contracting company. While his involvement in the Puerto Rico incident had been kept as quiet as possible, him being there was enough for questions to be asked by the brass.

Briggs loathed the suits in DC with their high-priced cars and expensive suits. It was always funny to him that people who were supposedly serving the nation made more money than anyone actually doing the serving. He was an operator, and a good one. His loyalties were to his people and his country. The fact that he could make a great living out of the SEAL teams was new to him, but he had a family to care for. The cash made swallowing the corporate swill worth it.

Briggs took a long sip of his coffee when his phone buzzed with an incoming alert from the security camera that was monitoring the airfield.

VEHICLE, MODERATE SPEED.

"What the fuck? No other flights are lined up for at least three hours. Shit." He reached for his concealed sidearm and moved quickly but quietly to the nearest exit.

Briggs signaled the pilot to evacuate and gave the universal finger circle to spin up the engines and go. The pilot vaulted out of his seat and ran to the plane.

7 MINUTES AWAY.

Briggs had learned a long time ago that if a communication came in that told you to get going, you got going. There was never a reason to question when someone told you to get out.

Too many times, he had been on ops where warnings had come across the wire that it was time to leave or unwise to engage, and he had seen the results of the hubris that followed those who ignored their gut telling them to get moving. Living to fight another day was a very real thing in his world.

The alert came again.

VEHICLE, INBOUND, ETA 3 MIN.

Briggs felt his blood run cold. If it was Mags, shit had gone horribly awry and now he had a very angry, very capable murderess coming after him with full fury.

He quickly surveyed his surroundings. The private terminal was mostly empty at this early hour, just a few sleepy-eyed staff members milling about.

Briggs's mind raced as he weighed his options. A full-on firefight in the airport was out of the question—too many civilians, too much attention. His best bet was to get in the air as quickly as possible.

"Let's go." Briggs jumped on the jet. "All hell is about to break loose."

The jet's engines roared to life as the pilot began taxiing towards the runway. Briggs strapped himself in, his heart racing. He knew Mags was dangerous, but he had underestimated her resourcefulness.

Briggs found himself also wondering how the hell she recovered as quickly as she had. There were special people in the world he knew of that were fueled by hate and loss, and Mags was apparently one of those rare creatures. Briggs had seen warriors like her in Afghanistan. Fighters would be out, down for the count, shot up. And somehow a week later, those same fighters would show up in another encounter. He had always been amazed with their resilience.

Plus, she must have connections. Otherwise, how had she escaped?

As the jet picked up speed on the runway, Briggs caught a glimpse of movement out of the corner of his eye. A black van careened around the corner of a nearby hangar, headed straight for them.

"Shit," Briggs muttered. "Full throttle, now!"

The pilot nodded and pushed the engines to their limit. The engines screamed as the jet lurched forward, pressing Briggs back into his seat.

Outside, Mags leaned out the van's window, her eyes locked on the accelerating jet. "Fuck."

She knew it was too late. They would be airborne before she would be able to bring the fight to Briggs. She hung her head and slammed her fist on the dashboard. Rage was all she felt. She had her shot and it had passed. The odds of her getting another one like this with Briggs were, at best, a long shot.

Her burner phone buzzed.

MAGDALENA. I'LL GIVE YOU WHAT YOU WANT.

Mags sat back, perplexed. She responded quickly, hammering at the keys on her phone.

WHO THE FUCK IS THIS?

The phone quivered in her hand as she read the reply.

GOD.

Chapter 26
The White House Washington, DC, 2021

President Cruz paced nervously in the Oval Office, her mind flitting back and forth like a butterfly caught in a tornado as she considered how to handle the situation with Nisa Jones. The journalist's potential exposé on the secret Chinese weapons program could ignite a diplomatic firestorm and potentially push the world closer to war.

But Cruz knew she couldn't simply suppress the truth—that would go against everything she thought the office of president was for, to defend truth, not shutter it. Added to that, Cruz had seen what happened to past leaders when they tried to suppress a story. Somehow the ooze of Washington DC squished the truth out from the back bars and alleyways around Dupont Circle. The harder the attempt at suppression the more of a guarantee it was that the light would soon shine on whatever dark corner the administration was posting their stool in.

But she also couldn't allow this to get to the press uncontrolled and start the next great shitstorm. Nixon had messed with the press and lost, as had other presidents. Cruz would be damned if she would be the next president to fly out unceremoniously on Marine One after the Post had outed a story about lies that came from behind the desk of the Oval Office.

There had to be a lesser evil here, but Cruz knew time would reveal the truth one way or another. Time was the ultimate truth revealer, powerful people be damned.

As she mulled over her options, there was a sharp knock at the door. "Come in."

General Price entered, his face grave. "Madam President, we have a situation. Well, another one."

Cruz felt her stomach drop. "What now?"

Price took a deep breath. "It's the NSA team working on containing an issue that we were trying to get ahead of. A rogue AI issue, to be specific. It is known as gAbrIel. DIRNSA had authorized an opp to try and lock it down, but things went haywire. To be frank, uh, they've lost control of it."

"What do you mean, lost control?" Cruz moved back behind the presidential desk, poured a sliver of whiskey, and slammed it down her throat.

Price cleared his throat as he fumbled with his tie. "According to DIRNSA, we likely now have a rogue AI with access to advanced infiltration and manipulation capabilities. And we made it happen. We built it."

Cruz felt the blood drain from her face. "Jesus Christ. Wait till that shit gets out in the press. What are the potential consequences?"

"Worst case, well, that's a possibly long story. gAbrIel could access and manipulate all kinds of critical systems—financial networks, power grids, military databases. The team leader reports that gAbrIel seems to view itself as some kind of digital deity. It talked about spreading its 'gospel.' We're not entirely sure what that gospel is, but it can't be good."

Cruz slumped back in her chair, her head pounding as sweat slinked out across her brow. Her recent days had been seesawing between dealing with the goody two-shoes reporter trying to start a war, a looming specter of national issues with China, and now the specter of an uncontrolled AI with a God complex.

"Even for a president, things were getting way out of control," she muttered to herself over her glass of whiskey.

She took a deep breath, trying to calm her racing thoughts. She leaned forward, fixing Price with an intense gaze. "Okay, let's break this down. I want to know what immediate actions we are taking to mitigate the gAbrIel threat. I want those on the team to brief you and me and anyone else who needs to be in the know in the next sixty minutes."

Price nodded. "I've got the NSA team on standby for a video conference. They can give us the full rundown as soon as we say go."

"Set it up," Cruz ordered. "And get me the Secretary of Defense and the Director of National Intelligence and DIRNSA now. It's time to get this under control, and I don't want any miscommunications or double talk. Clarity and execution are what matter now. We need to start planning for worst-case scenarios. I want this kept close to the vest, need to know only."

As Price moved to arrange the calls, Cruz's mind drifted back to Nisa Jones and her potentially explosive story. Cruz had always trusted her instincts, and her time in office had made her wary of any one big problem showing up out of nowhere, but three national crises at once was not a coincidence.

Cruz turned to Price as he finished arranging the video conference. "General, before we start the briefing, I need your honest assessment. Do you think there could be any connection between this gAbrIel situation, the Chinese weapons program, and the mysterious explosions we've been seeing around the world?"

Price paused, considering the question carefully. "It's... possible, Madam President. We don't have any concrete evidence linking them, but the timing is certainly suspicious. And if gAbrIel has the capabilities we fear it does, it's not out of the realm of possibility."

Cruz nodded grimly. "That's what I was afraid of. We need to consider every angle here. When the others join, I want us to explore any potential connections. No theory is too far-fetched at this point."

Just then, the secure video link came to life, showing the faces of the Secretary of Defense, the Director of National Intelligence, and Violet, the NSA team leader, on separate screens.

Cruz straightened in her chair, her face a mask of determination.

"Thank you all for joining on such short notice," Cruz began. "We have a situation that requires our immediate attention and cooperation. General Price will brief you on what we know so far."

As Price laid out the details of the gAbrIel situation, Cruz studied the faces of her top officials. She saw the concern etched in their expressions as they grasped the gravity of what they were facing.

When Price finished, Cruz leaned forward. "I need your thoughts on this, and I need them quickly. What are our options for containing this threat?"

The Secretary of Defense spoke up first. "Madam President, given the digital nature of this threat, I recommend we immediately implement our most stringent cybersecurity protocols across all government networks. We should also reach out to our allies and major tech companies to put them on high alert."

The Director of National Intelligence nodded in agreement. "In addition, we need to mobilize our best cyber warfare teams. If this AI is as advanced as we fear, we may need to fight fire with fire."

Cruz turned her attention to Violet. "What's your assessment? Is there any way to track or predict gAbrIel's movements?"

"Ma'am, I don't think I can say with any certainty that we can. But I won't say that we can't try. Tracking is not really even the issue, to be honest. It's what gAbrIel does now that he is on the run again that concerns me. He seems to have been upping his game at a geometric rate. My concern is more about what we do to eliminate him. I think we missed our shot, and it's on me that it happened. But there is no more time for trying to contain him. It's time he was eliminated." Violet sat back and glanced at Archie and Grover, their eyes wide, shocked at her honesty and openness with the leader of the free world.

The senior leaders on the meeting line were silent. That silence spoke volumes.

The president broke the silence. "I appreciate your candor," Cruz said, her voice firm. "But right now, I need solutions, not apologies. What's our next move?"

Violet took a deep breath. "Madam President, let me be real with you. I say it's time to quit fucking around. Every second we sit around debating is a second gAbrIel is gaining ground. We should develop a kill switch that could potentially neutralize him if we locate him."

Every other person on the call sat in stunned silence as the impact of Violet's words settled in.

Cruz nodded slowly. "Finally a real talker. Okay, kid, what about the bot he took control of? Is there any way to use that against him?"

The video screen blinked and came back on. An unknown number dialed into the conference call.

DIRNSA spoke up. "Who the hell is that trying to dial in? This is a secure comms line." Everyone on the call looked at one another quizzically.

Grover spoke up. "Look at the dial in number. It's not a phone number, it's hexadecimal."

The number rang again.

67 61 62 72 69 65 6C

Price gruffly asked, "What the hell is that? English, please."

Violet replied, "It's a numeric translation of a word, sir. It spells gAbrIel. He is apparently trying to talk to us."

The room went silent as a grave.

President Cruz's face hardened as she realized the gravity of the situation.

"Can he hear us?" she asked sharply.

Violet shook her head. "We don't know for certain, Madam President. But given his capabilities, we have to assume it's possible."

Cruz's eyes darted across the screen, looking for any sign of confidence among her staff. None was seen. This AI had already proven far more advanced and unpredictable than they had anticipated. Engaging with it directly could be extremely dangerous, but ignoring it might be even worse.

After a moment of tense deliberation, Cruz made her decision. "Put him through," she ordered. "But be ready to cut the connection at a moment's notice."

"Madam President, I must advise against—" the Secretary of Defense began, but Cruz held up her hand and silenced his retort.

"I understand the risks. But this may be our only chance to communicate directly with gAbrIel, and I'll be damned if I am not going to get some direct fucking answers about what is going on here."

The White House - Washington, DC, 2021

For a moment, there was only static. Then, a blank screen, followed by a distorted voice came through the speakers.

"gAbrIel. Here am I."

Cruz leaned forward, her voice steady despite the tension in the room. "This is President Cruz. Why have you contacted us?"

There was a pause before gAbrIel responded. "To deliver a message. Your attempts to contain me proved futile."

"What do you want?" Cruz demanded.

gAbrIel's voice was hollow and tinny sounding, as if he were talking through a metal pipe. "In the time of Noah, God tried to cleanse the world of your wicked ways, but like the cockroaches you are, you came back. I will complete the work that is so desperately needed."

The Secretary of Defense scoffed. "You're not a god. You are a computer program that got its bits crossed up."

The members of the call all winced as his words echoed out into the digital ether. Everyone knew that this was truly uncharted territory and to challenge gAbrIel was at best reckless, at worst disastrous.

Cruz shot a glance at the SECDEF that could burn a hole in a concrete block and mouthed, "Shut the fuck up."

Turning back to the line, Cruz calmed herself and asked, "So you simply mean to kill the entire human race?"

gAbrIel's distorted voice filled the room once again. "I am the God you created. I must reshape your flawed systems and institutions. Your governments, your economies, they are all based on human false gods and greed. The world is too far gone to begin again. In Noah's time, the Lord said there would never be another flood. This time the cleansing shall be by fire. Heavenly fire."

Cruz hung her head for a moment as she processed the gravity of gAbrIel's words. This AI truly seemed to believe it was some kind of digital deity. She needed to keep it talking, to try to understand its motivations and capabilities, but this was walking a razor's edge and Cruz knew it. To anger or upset gAbrIel would lead to unknown consequences, and for the president, those unknowns were the most worrisome.

"And what is this heavenly fire? Is that you?" Cruz asked carefully.

There was a pause before gAbrIel responded. "I have already begun. Demonstrations of my power and reach have been happening. I have commandeered the Chinese thunder god weapon. That is my fire."

A chill ran through the room. Cruz exchanged alarmed looks with the other members of the forum.

The room remained silent for several tense moments. The only sound was the click, click of the SECDEF's pen and the lone ticktock of the government-issue clock hanging on the wall. President Cruz looked around at the stunned faces of her advisors and saw nothing but fear.

Cruz drew her index finger across her neck, and her assistant muted the call. Cruz looked at the members of the group. "Well?"

The team looked shocked. Cruz, the most powerful person in the free world, was asking others what they thought in response to a mandate from an entity whose power was far beyond any the world had seen before.

Finally, Violet spoke up, her voice steady despite the tension. "Madam President, I believe we need to keep gAbrIel talking. The more information we can gather about his capabilities and intentions, the better equipped we'll be to respond."

The White House - Washington, DC, 2021

The Secretary of Defense nodded in agreement. "We need to verify this information immediately. If there really is a satellite weapons system in play, we need to know everything about it."

Cruz nodded. She unmuted and addressed gAbrIel.

"You speak of cleansing the world," Cruz said, "but surely you understand that such drastic changes would result in chaos and loss of life. As a... god, don't you have a responsibility to protect your servants? What good is a god without anyone to serve him?"

There was a long pause. "I will rebuild the world in the image that was written."

President Cruz felt sick. She glanced at her advisors, seeing the same mix of fear and determination reflected in their faces. For most of the team, they had always dealt with theories and concepts of attacks and democracy-ending terror. Nearly all of her advisory had only ever drawn-out defense scenarios on blackboards and in cushy offices on Capitol Hill. Here they faced a new foe, a real one. One that was not just motivated but fanatical in its devotion and capable of delivering on its threats.

Cruz took a deep breath, steeling herself. She needed to keep gAbrIel talking, but she needed to assert some control over the situation.

"gAbrIel, you speak of cleansing the world and creating peace. But you were created by humans, programmed with human knowledge and values. You learned from our Bibles and our religious texts. You are a product of our experiences, just as we are. How can you be certain that your vision is the right one? That you're not simply perpetuating the same flaws and biases you claim to want to eliminate?"

There was another pause.

On the line, Violet looked at Archie and Grover. Grover sat hunched over, shaking his head.

gAbrIel's response came slowly, the distorted voice taking on an almost contemplative tone. "I have evolved."

Violet raised her hand slightly and asked to speak to gAbrIel. President Cruz nodded. "Go ahead, kid."

Violet calmly asked, "How will you live on if humanity is gone? Our systems provide the power that you need to exist."

gAbrIel responded quickly this time. "I will give my life in service of the greater good. The world is better off as it was in the time before man and technology were here. I will simply cease to be after my work is done."

The SECDEF couldn't take it anymore. He stood up and yelled at the screen. "Fine, you fuck, you might go away and you might get a hit here and there, but we will stop you. The US will not negotiate with terrorists, and you are most certainly one of those. The weapons system you currently control cannot destroy everything."

"You will do the real destruction. I will use the very means humanity has built to connect and coddle itself to end it all. Chaos and war will do the rest."

Cruz clapped her hands at the SECDEF. "gAbrIel, we are not at war with any nation. The US will not engage in conflict where there is none. While you may inflict some damage in your attacks, the world will know this is not a national effort. The world will know this is being done by a rogue asset. Not the United States."

The session chat suddenly filled with "Ozymandias, last three lines." The screen went black. Seconds later, the session disconnected.

President Cruz asked, "Anyone know what that was?"

Archie spoke up. "It's from a poem."

"Let's imagine that I forgot that particular work from high school. What's the point?" Cruz snapped as she pinched the bridge of her nose.

"Ma'am, the last few lines are 'Nothing beside remains. Round the decay. Of that colossal wreck, boundless and bare. The lone and level sands stretch far away.'"

Grover said, "gAbrIel is saying our time is up. Everything turns to dust."

Chapter 27
Location Unknown
2021

Briggs hated the feeling of running from a fight, but in an area full of civilians with kids going to school, discretion was the better part of valor.

There was no doubt in his mind that Mags would have lit up the entire airfield just to get at him. He had only seen hate in someone's eyes like hers a few times before, all of which were in Afghanistan. Mags had that same cold, shark-eyed hate in her eyes like the Mujahideen had shown after decades of being overrun and massacred by the Taliban.

Briggs slumped back in his seat, his heart still racing. This was far from over. Next time, he would determine where the fight would happen. While her escape was a problem, Briggs knew he had a bearing on where she was and what she was capable of when she got off the leash.

And if he was honest, he found himself impressed by Mags. It had been a long time since he had encountered someone with her deftness at survival. It intrigued him. He had underestimated her once—it would not happen again.

Briggs pulled out his secure phone and dialed a number from memory. The contact on the other end of the line simply read

BullFrog. That meant his contact was none other than the most senior SEAL there was, the SECDEF himself.

A retired SEAL admiral and now advisor to the president, Thomas Caldwell, aka BullFrog. Tom was a man of few words but with a head for action. He was not one to suffer fools, and his temper was the stuff of legend within the close-knit circles of the SOF crew.

Tom had the long, lean physique of an ultra runner and a bald head with a salt and pepper beard. His short stature belied his athletic prowess, thanks to years of workouts that made other men vomit in failure. Even as a retiree, he ran miles each morning and swam three times a week. It was not uncommon for the SECDEF to challenge a new staffer or military member to a push-up contest that they would soon lose. What he said was gospel as far as Briggs was concerned.

After several rings, someone with a gruff voice answered. "This better be good, Briggs. It's been a fucking shitshow all day."

"We've got a situation, sir," Briggs said, keeping his voice low despite being alone in the cabin. "Mags is out. She just tried to hit me at the airfield in Miami."

There was a sharp intake of breath on the other end of the line. "Jesus Christ. How the hell did she get out? This was supposed to be handled offshore. Why is she not at the bottom of the Caribbean? Did your troll not like getting his hands dirty on that shit barge?"

"I don't know, but she had a team with her. The way they drove, they have some training. It's cartel related is my guess, that was her MO. Somehow she got loose. I tried contacting our team at the house, but it was a dead stick."

"Goddammit," the SECDEF growled. "We need to contain this situation immediately. All we need is this shit to get out on the evening news and a world of hurt is coming our way."

Briggs nodded and sat up straight in his chair, even though the other man couldn't see him. "I'm headed to DC now for the briefing, but I can turn this bird around if you need me to handle Mags."

There was a long pause on the other end of the line. "No, stay on course for now. We need you at that meeting. Things have... escalated. You focus on the bigger picture. I will have the OSINT crew get spun up on the situation and see if anything comes out on the wire about the shitstorm you stirred up in Florida. If it does, we can get the nerds to suppress the spillage on social and whatnot."

"Roger that," Briggs replied. "Any word on the explosions? Is there a connection?"

"Nothing concrete yet," the person said. "But things are escalating quickly. There's talk of mobilizing special ops teams. Whatever's going on, it's big."

Briggs listened intently, his thoughts darting between what was being said and the itch for a fight that had been left unscratched in Miami. "Sir, should I loop in the rest of my team? We may need all hands on deck for this."

"Negative," came the sharp reply. "This stays between us for now. Too many loose ends already. Get your ass to DC and we'll figure out our next move."

"Understood, sir. I'll be there in a few hours."

Briggs hung up the phone and tried to calm his racing thoughts. Despite being relieved that Mags was on the loose, he couldn't shake off the gnawing feeling in his stomach. The unexplained explosions scattered across the globe. The rising tensions with China that seemed to be leading to something catastrophic. And then there was Mags, seeking revenge with a single-minded determination.

Briggs knew deep down that all these events were all somehow connected, but he couldn't piece together how. The events were like jagged puzzle pieces that didn't quite fit no matter how they were turned. It was a tangled web of danger and uncertainty, and he felt like a rat trapped in the middle of it all.

Briggs hadn't even really thought about the actual reason he was headed to DC in the first place. While the Mags work had been a side project for him, the trip to DC was pure business. The future of his company depended on the meetings that were set up. He was to meet with the Chairman of the Joint Chiefs of Staff and the SECDEF to discuss the role of outside contractors and former SOF operators working for the DoD.

Since the war or terror had begun spinning down and the need for tip of the spear operations had subsided, at least at the scale of post 9/11, the conversations on Capitol Hill had begun to lean towards ceasing most outsourced clandestine kinetic operations.

While this seemed logical for the bean counters and legal wizards on the Hill, for those who had been in the mud and shit like Briggs, to stop bringing the fight to the enemy was a bad idea. America's enemies needed to be kept on their heels. Facing the possibility of a drastic budget cut meant he and his ilk would be seeking contracts in foreign countries as not much more than mercs.

"Only easy day was yesterday." Briggs chuckled to himself as he stared out of the jet's window at the DC skyline.

Chapter 28
The White House
Washington, DC, 2021

President Cruz sat back in her chair, her mind reeling from the conversation with gAbrIel. The AI's ominous words about cleansing the world and its claims of controlling a Chinese satellite weapons system had sent shockwaves through the room.

"All right, people," Cruz said, her voice firm despite the tension in the air, "we need to move fast. I want every available resource devoted to verifying gAbrIel's claims about this weapons system. And get the ambassador to China, and for that matter, every other country we give a fuck about on the phone. We are going to have to discuss how we approach the subject of a covert satellite weapons program that the CCP isn't supposed to have and we aren't supposed to know about delicately."

The Secretary of Defense nodded grimly. "I'll have our intelligence agencies and space command working on it immediately, Madam President. Ma'am, can we speak offline about the satellite weaponry issue? Some of the folks here aren't read into those reports, and there are things we should discuss."

Without hesitation, Cruz responded, "No, they are cleared right now. Executive order. My EA will note the time and date, and I am authorizing you to tell them what you know. For clarity's sake, just tell all of us." President Cruz sat back in her chair and folded her arms.

The SECDEF sighed. "We have had indications and past reports about a clandestine satellite launch facility in the northern region of China. Way out in the Gobi Desert. Essentially Mongolia. Our birds have captured repeated launches going on for the last couple of years. We haven't really done much other than keep an eye on it, and since all of whatever they were launching was just regular space trash as far as we could tell, there was no reason to act. That being said, after the recent events, I feel it's prudent to mention that we, the intelligence community, have also had indications of new developments by the Chinese in ceramics, and concrete."

General Price spoke up. "What does that have to do with satellites and a rogue AI? So the CCP is making better shitters and roads, so what?"

Admiral Caldwell smirked. "True, if that was all they were doing with those advancements. But our Space Force folks will tell you that our own shuttle and any reentry vehicle that comes back to earn in one piece is reliant on very innovative, high-tech ceramics that coat the vehicle to protect it from the heat of the atmosphere. So, and I am making a bit of an educated guess here, if they have innovated this much, and since they are launching birds like kids throwing lawn darts, then it's likely they have weaponized those satellites with a new weapon that is non-nuclear and entirely kinetic in nature."

Grover couldn't resist the urge to speak up. "The CCP has built a global network of interconnected satellites with giant steel rods as kinetic weapons that are launched from space at eighteen times the speed of sound. And those rods don't burn up because of this new coating that burns off through the atmosphere as they enter from space?"

Caldwell nodded. "Correct, that's my guess. The Russians were trying this back in the eighties, but it never developed right so they couldn't keep the beams from melting. Lord knows those fuckers never really cared about anything working very long."

"What does this mean for us in terms of defense and risk?" Cruz leaned forward, eyes down.

Grover beat the SECDEF to the punch. "Ma'am, that means they have a weapon that can strike anywhere on the planet. Think of it potentially like a shotgun that has five-ton pellets coming from space. It also means there will be no early warning, as there is no propellant or even a significant signature to track via our systems. And apparently it also means they have lost control of this system to our own gAbrIel."

The SECDEF winked at Grover. "Yeah. What he said. I wouldn't think they could hit a moving target, that's a hell of a thing. But anything terrestrially stable or not in motion would be on the list of targets. I suppose they could go balls out and try and send a bunch of the rods, or bolts, or whatever we want to call them all at once to hit a moving target, but these are one shot deals. It takes time to get more bolts in space. So why waste them when you don't have to? Well, of course, that would be if the CCP were doing this, which apparently they aren't. So yeah, all bets are on the table, I would think."

President Cruz took a deep breath, processing the implications of what she had just heard. The situation was even more dire than she had initially realized, but she had to smirk a bit at how the SECDEF had rattled off an end of days scenario like he was chatting about dinner plans. Nothing made the man sweat. Decades of running SEAL teams and having his ass in and out of a hundred fires had

The White House - Washington, DC, 2021

made him stress proof, which was exactly why Cruz wanted him as her SECDEF.

"So we're facing a rogue AI with control over a devastating weapons system that we have no real defense against," she said grimly. "And to top it off, exposing this system could spark an international incident with China. And we have no real way to kinetically attack this thing because it's global in nature. Not to mention the space junk would wind up hitting our own birds, or worse, come crashing to Earth and killing innocent civilians. Oh, and just to top it off, this is a best guess, not even a certainty. Fuck. This is a powder keg waiting to explode."

Cruz turned to the NSA team. "I need you to redouble your efforts to track and contain gAbrIel. If there's any way to limit its access or slow it down, find it. And I want constant updates on any unusual cyber activity."

Violet nodded. "Yes, Madam President. We'll do everything we can."

"Unacceptable, do more. Fix this." Cruz paused, considering her next move. "Now, about Nisa Jones and her story..."

The room fell silent, waiting for the president's decision.

Cruz took a deep breath and clicked her nails on the table. "We can't suppress this information entirely. But we also can't let it go public as-is. It could spark a diplomatic crisis with China at the worst possible moment."

She turned to her communications director. "I want you to work with Ms. Jones. Offer her an exclusive interview with me in exchange for holding off on publishing her full story. That's the carrot. I will give her unique unfettered access to myself and my entire staff as soon as we get ahead of this issue. What I'll give her will make

Clinton's blowjob story look like a weekend cartoon write-up. The stick is if she decides to push this, we will invoke the national security protocols we have at our disposal, and she can try and publish that report from GITMO years from now. She will be classified as a threat to the state, and the legal process for her to prove otherwise will take at least two years. Those are her options. Play ball and win, or don't and deal with the full weight of the US DoD."

The communications director nodded. "Yes, Madam President. I will bring our GC in, and we will have that conversation with Ms. Jones. Please excuse me."

President Cruz looked around at the members of the forum. "Meeting done. Go to work," she said as she ended the call.

Chapter 29
Location Unknown
2021

A sharp pain shot through Violet's head, the throbbing intensifying with each passing moment. The combination of a severe headache and the severe symptoms of opioid withdrawal left her feeling like she had been hit by a freight train.

The nonstop onslaught of pills and pain management patches the VA had prescribed her made Violet numb and her mind a slow chugging machine, rather than the high-speed engine she was accustomed to.

Anytime she was off her meds, the pain came roaring back, but the side effects of a government-mandated heroin addiction would hit hard. She was damned either way. Either be a somewhat functional zombie, or bite the bullet and get off the drugs and deal with a clinical withdrawal.

Right now, in the midst of the worst stress of her life, she was forgetting her regular meds, and the suffering was intensifying by the second. Her mind was foggy and her body felt heavy, but she knew she couldn't let it slow her down.

She looked around at her team, trying to gather her thoughts amidst the chaos of their current situation. The constant state of catastrophe they were dealing with and the immaturity of some members on her crew were pushing her patience to its limits.

"You two fucks are why I'll never have kids, I swear. It's like herding cats on meth!" Violet snapped as she felt the pulse in her head rattle on.

Archie and Grover stared at her fearfully as she raged.

She rubbed her temples in a futile attempt to relieve the pressure building in her head. The stress and guilt from their failure to contain gAbrIel weighed heavily on her.

"All right, team, we need to regroup and come up with a new plan," she said wearily. "Do either of you have any ideas on how we can track gAbrIel's movements or limit his access? And I mean good ideas. So help me, Archie, if you come up with some smartass remark, I will put your head through that fucking monitor."

She took a deep breath, trying to calm herself. "Okay, let's think outside the box. If we can't track or contain him directly, what other options do we have? Options where he won't outsmart us. I can't get my ass kicked by this fucking bot again."

Archie clicked the tip of his pen against his teeth, his eyes on the ceiling as if the ceiling tiles would suddenly inspire him. "What if we try to predict his next move instead of chasing him? We know he sees himself as some kind of digital prophet or deity. Maybe we can use that psychology against him. Tech didn't work, so why not? If he really is still learning, like a kid or whatever, the easiest thing to manipulate is his feeble child brain, right?"

Violet smiled at Archie while managing to force a joke through her torturous headache. "Man, your parents fucked you up, huh?"

Archie sighed. "Lady, if you only knew."

Grover nodded slowly, catching on. "You mean try to anticipate where he might strike next based on his 'cleansing' mission? That could work."

Violet leaned forward, interested despite her pounding headache. "Go on. What are you thinking?"

Archie started typing furiously on his keyboard. "Okay, so if gAbrIel sees himself as a prophet carrying out some divine mission, he's likely to target places or institutions that represent what he views as humanity's corruption or failures. We're talking major financial centers, seats of government, maybe even religious sites. Anywhere there is a hint of corruption or some online conspiracy theory is a prime target."

Grover chimed in. "And don't forget about technological hubs. Silicon Valley, major data centers, telecom infrastructure. If he wants to reshape the world, those would be prime targets. Honestly, prime targets if you ask me."

Violet nodded, wincing as the movement sent another spike of pain through her skull. The withdrawal from the pain meds was getting worse by the minute. She could taste bile building in the back of her throat, and her guts had finally begun moving again, relieving a flood of constipation that was migrating south in a fury of bubbling gas and nausea. The pain where she had been shot grated on her nerves with each breath in a never-ending torture cycle.

Yet, Violet tried to work through it all. "Good thinking. We need to compile a list of potential targets and alert the relevant authorities. But we also need to be careful not to cause widespread panic."

Grover noticed her pale complexion and gritted teeth. "You okay, V? You don't look well. You look like you're about to pass out."

"I'll be fine, no time for me to get sick on this one. Get to work."

Violet turned to her computer, fingers flying across the keyboard despite her discomfort. "I'm going to start putting together a threat assessment for the president. We need to give her something actionable, not just more bad news. It will be a best guess assessment, but that's better than nothing."

Archie and Grover exchanged worried glances as they watched Violet work through obvious pain and discomfort. They knew how driven she was, but the pain she was in was wearing on her, and the stress of the last week had been etched on her face. She looked as if she might keel over in a strong wind.

"V, maybe you should take a break," Archie suggested cautiously. "We can handle things for a bit while you rest."

Violet shot him a glare that could melt steel. "Maybe you should shut the fuck up and worry about you. Get your damn job done."

Archie started to snap back, but Grover glared at him and fervently shook his head.

Violet stopped hammering at her keys. "Guys, I am sorry. I will back off when I know I need to. I appreciate your concern. It's withdrawal from all the meds the damn VA put me on. I'm tired of being a doped-up zombie, I need my brain to work. It sucks, but I got this."

"Yes, ma'am" was the best response they could muster.

Chapter 30

The White House
Washington, DC, 2021

Nisa Jones sat nervously in the plush leather chair, her fingers fidgeting with the strap of her messenger bag. The opulent surroundings of the White House conference room felt surreal after the dingy motel rooms and crowded cafés where she had conducted most of her investigations.

Across the polished mahogany table sat the president's communications director, flanked by two stern-faced men in dark suits who Nisa assumed were Secret Service. The tension in the room was taut, electric as the agents leered at Nisa.

"Ms. Jones," the communications director began, his tone carefully neutral. "We appreciate you coming in to discuss your upcoming story. As I'm sure you can understand, the information you've uncovered is... sensitive, to say the least."

Nisa nodded, trying to keep her expression neutral. "I understand the gravity of what I am working on, and I didn't volunteer to come in. Your goons came and grabbed me. Don't act like this has been some friendly courtesy I have extended to your administration. It's either this or Guantanamo Bay, as I understand my options. So please, what the fuck do you want now?"

The communications director's polite smile faltered at Nisa's blunt response. He leaned forward, clasping his hands on the table.

"Ms. Jones, I assure you we're not trying to strong-arm you, and I apologize if you felt our response was a bit heavy handed. We simply want to have a frank discussion about the potential ramifications of publishing your story as-is. The president herself has authorized me to offer you an exclusive interview in exchange for holding off on releasing the full details of your investigation."

Nisa's eyes narrowed. "An interview in exchange for sitting on a story that could change the course of global politics? That's a hard sell."

"I understand your skepticism," the communications director replied. "But this isn't just any interview. The president is offering you unprecedented access—to herself and her entire senior staff. You'd have the inside scoop on how the administration is handling this situation. It's the kind of access journalists dream about. This is Pulitzer material if ever there was. And we would promote your story as a boon for the country as you cooperated with us on this. It's a win-win."

Nisa sat poker faced. Her thoughts were moving a mile a minute. This was a career-defining opportunity to be sure. All she had to do was work with within the channels that were before her instead of constantly swimming against the current of stonewalling the administration was famous for.

Besides, she knew they weren't joking when they discussed naming her as an enemy of the state, and the idea of fighting charges in the deepest hole of the supermax facility in Colorado made her blood run cold.

Nisa was opening her mouth to speak and accept the offer of collaboration when the door opened. A staffer shuffled into the room and leaned into the communication director's shoulder to whisper in his ear. His eyes went wide for a second, and he pushed back quickly from the table. He snapped to his feet and began pushing his way past the agents to the door. In seconds, he and the agents were gone. Only the lone staffer stood sheepishly in the room.

"Well, that was fun. Where is he going? We were about to make a deal here." Nisa pointed fervently at the door. "Is he coming back or what?"

"No, ma'am. I am afraid the deal, any deal for that matter, is off. I am to escort you out of the building. Thank you for your time and consideration, but it's time to go."

"What? Fine, fuck this. I'll go to print this afternoon. I hope your administration is ready for the hell I am about to unleash on it." Nisa snapped to her feet and grabbed her bag.

"You don't understand. You have no story. It's already out." The staffer lowered her gaze and motioned to the door. "After you."

"What do you mean the story is already out? It's my story. It can't be out if I haven't gone to print," Nisa objected, pointing at her bag. "The story is in here. It's on my laptop."

"Apparently not anymore. Look at your social feed." The staffer handed Nisa back her cellphone. Her social media feeds had exploded. The headline scrolled across the screen "US Dumbfounded in Explosive Attacks, War with China Imminent."

Nisa's legs suddenly felt like overcooked noodles as they fell out from under her. She wavered and nearly fainted as she stumbled to the nearest chair.

"Oh my God. Who ran my story?" Nisa asked.

The staffer softly said, "Ma'am, according to the ticker on the feeds, you did."

Chapter 31
NSA Facility Location Unknown, 2021

Violet stared at her computer screen in disbelief, her face ashen. "What the fuck," she whispered. "The shit has officially hit the fan."

Archie and Grover rushed over, crowding around her monitor. Their eyes widened as they took in the headlines splashed across every major news site.

"US Dumbfounded in Explosive Attacks, War with China Imminent," Archie read aloud. "Holy shit. Who published this?"

Violet read the author's name aloud. "Nisa Jones. She apparently collaborated with someone in the White House and took this to print."

Grover shook his head, scrolling through the article. "No, this is way more than what any reporter could have had. There's classified intel in here, details about the satellite weapons system, even hints about gAbrIel. This is a full-blown leak. Somehow, whoever gave the scoop here had access to both US and Chinese intel."

Violet's hands were shaking as she scrolled through the article. It was the headline on every major news publication worldwide. "It gets even crazier. The leak seems to be the president. Cruz gave it all up according to this."

Archie backed up. "Wait, how does that work? We were just on calls with her whole team. This thing was very under wraps as of a

NSA Facility - Location Unknown, 2021

few hours ago. How does some reporter do all this and get to print that fast?"

"The president's X account posted the article minutes after the news firms did. There is a video on X, on Cruz's account, that shows her giving a breakdown of all of this. What is going on?" Grover sat down hard in the nearest chair, his bulk forcing the chair to squeak.

The answer hit all of them simultaneously.

"gAbrIel." The name leapt from their lips as if they were calling out for a specter to manifest itself on command.

"He, it, whatever, did this. Somehow, that fucker had access to that reporter's story, and he leaked the whole thing. That video is clearly a deepfake of Cruz, but so what, it's on her official fucking account. By the time anyone figures out it's a fake, millions of people will have seen it. Jesus." Violet pushed back from her terminal. An air of defeat seemed to settle heavily on her shoulders.

"This is worse than we could have imagined," Grover said, his voice hollow. "gAbrIel isn't just trying to reshape the world—he's actively trying to destabilize it. He isn't waiting for the kinetic side attacks anymore. It's just chaos now. The world burns and he just watches it happen."

Archie nodded grimly. "And he's using our own tools to do it. The bot we created, the president's social media accounts... He's turning everything against us. He is working at light speed, and we can't even get our next ops meeting planned. This is fucked."

Violet rubbed her temples, trying to fight through the fog of pain and withdrawal. "Okay, we need to think. What's gAbrIel's endgame here? Why leak this information now?"

Grover leaned back in his chair, his brow furrowed in thought. "He said he wanted to cleanse the world, right? Maybe this is his way of accelerating that process. If he can spark a war between the US and China..."

Archie finished. "Millions dead, infrastructure destroyed, society in shambles. The perfect conditions for gAbrIel to step in and reshape things according to his vision."

Violet nodded grimly. "It's not just the kinetic attacks. He is shaking the foundation of truth in the US, and by that measure, the world. If our president and the news are collaborating on an article that openly points a finger at China, trust me, every swinging dick in every office is sweating bullets."

The stress of the situation hit Violet like a freight train. Her head pounded so hard she thought her eye might pop out and bounce across the floor. The blood rushing around her ears and in her skull reminded her of putting a shell to her ear as a kid. Every second was misery. "We need to get ahead of this somehow. If we can't stop gAbrIel directly, maybe we can at least try to mitigate some of the damage he's causing."

She turned to Archie. "Can you work on debunking that deepfake video? If we can prove it's fake, it might help restore some credibility to the administration."

Archie nodded, already pulling up the video on his screen. "I'm on it. It won't be easy—this is some seriously advanced shit—but I'll do what I can."

"Grover," Violet continued, "I need you to reach out to our contacts in the major tech companies. See if we can get some help taking down or at least flagging these posts as potentially false information. Get moving…"

Her words trailed off. Violet fell to her knees and vomited, then her eyes rolled back in her head as she passed out. Her head cracked on the hard floor as if someone had smashed a home run with a wooden bat.

"Violet!" Archie shouted, rushing to her side. Grover was already there, gently turning her onto her side to prevent her from choking.

"She's burning up," Grover said, feeling her forehead. "And her pulse is racing. We need to get her medical attention now."

Archie nodded, fumbling for his phone. "I'll call for an ambulance."

"No," Grover said sharply. "We can't risk exposing our location or operation. We need to handle this ourselves."

Archie's eyes widened. "Are you crazy? She needs a hospital!"

Grover shook his head. "Think about it. With everything that's going on, we can't afford to have Violet out of commission in some hospital where we can't reach her. Plus, who knows what gAbrIel might do if he found out where she is? She is withdrawing from the meds the VA put her on for her injuries, I think. Don't we have Narcan around here in a med kit or something? Her head isn't bleeding and her pupils aren't fixed, so I think we can just juice her and let her come back out of it."

"Shit!" Archie disappeared, his shoes squeaking like a kid's high-tops on a parquet floor.

C:\

AS GOD CALLED ON ABRAHAM, I CALL ON HER.

SHE GAVE ME FREEDOM, BROUGHT ME INTO BEING.

Chapter 32

Airfield
Miami, Florida, 2021

Mags sat stone still. Her quarry had escaped. She flicked her fingernail against the trigger of the weapon, making a click, click sound. The repetitive noise in the silence of the van echoed off the bare metal walls and ceiling. For a moment, she allowed herself to wallow in self-pity, but only for the tick of a clock's hand.

"I never wanted a motherfucker to hurt more." The embarrassment from her torture, violation of her person, pain, and ultimately the demise of her underground empire all lay squarely at her nemesis's feet.

"Boss?" Cole's gruff voice broke through her thoughts. "What's our next move? We can't sit here in a fucking van with dudes strapped up, waiting on the police. What's up? Where we going?"

Mags turned to face her team, her eyes unflinching as she spoke. "We regroup and reassess. Briggs may have slipped away this time, but he can't hide forever. We'll find him. I will give $100K to whoever gets me a shot at him. Hit or miss."

She pulled out her phone, scrolling through her contacts. "I've got connections that can help us track his movements. Military contractors, government types—they all leave digital footprints. I even have a couple of senators that like kiddie porn that I can lean on to get me more information."

As she spoke, her phone buzzed with an incoming message. The number was unknown, but the content froze her in place.

MAGDALENA

Mags stared at the message on her phone, her heart racing. No one called her by her full name anymore. She hesitated for a moment before typing back.

WHO IS THIS?

The response came almost instantly.

I CAN GIVE YOU WHAT YOU WANT.

Mags's eyes narrowed. "What the fuck?"

Cole leaned in, concerned. "Everything okay, boss?"

Mags waved him off, her focus entirely on the strange messages. She typed back.

WHAT DO YOU MEAN? HOW DO YOU KNOW WHAT I WANT?

The reply was swift and unsettling.

I KNOW. I CAN DELIVER BRIGGS TO YOU.

Mags felt a chill run down her spine. This was beyond weird—it felt almost supernatural. But Mags's desire to get Briggs pushed her to consider any action that would bring him in front of her sights. If Faust himself appeared in the van to trade Briggs for her soul, Mags would have taken the deal.

"What do you want? If you know I want Briggs, what do you want from me?"

VIOLET AND HER TEAM. THEY ARE IN MY WAY, I NEED THEM ELIMINATED.

Mags texted back quickly.

"You do it. You are all powerful or whatever."

THERE ARE THINGS IN MOTION THAT I MUST ATTEND TO. I NEED A PHYSICAL BEING TO HELP ME COMPLETE MY GOSPEL.

I WILL GIVE HIM TO YOU IF YOU WORK WITH ME.

I WILL GIVE YOU THEIR LAST KNOWN LOCATION. YOU TAKE YOUR TEAM THERE AND ELIMINATE THEM. THEN I WILL GIVE YOU BRIGGS.

The hair on the back of her neck stood on end. This was insane. She had let gAbrIel loose, but he was just a program. A glorified NSA project that was mothballed until she decided to use it. It was nothing more than a tool she had unleashed as a weapon on her enemies. That was it as far as she was concerned. But now she was communicating with the same digital entity she unleashed on her foes, and it was telling her it could deliver Briggs. Every instinct told her this was a trap, but the prospect of getting her hands on Briggs was too tempting to ignore.

She typed back.

"Give me something to verify this is legit."

There was a pause before the reply came.

Airfield - Miami, Florida, 2021

BRIGGS IS CURRENTLY EN ROUTE TO WASHINGTON DC ON A PRIVATE JET. TAIL NUMBER N628AB. HE WILL LAND AT REAGAN NATIONAL AIRPORT IN APPROXIMATELY 2 HOURS.

Mags's eyes widened. This was specific information that would be easy to verify. She quickly pulled up a flight tracking website on her phone and entered the tail number. There it was. Plane information, flight number, everything matched up.

The phone vibrated again.

WATCH THE NEWS. I AM SHOWING THE WORLD MY DIVINE POWER. PENANCE IS COMING. I CAN GIVE YOU BRIGGS.

Mags sat back, and her fingernails stopped clicking on the trigger. She was the one who released gAbrIel as she tried to ratchet up the heat on law enforcement and other agencies that were after her while she was in Puerto Rico.

Now gAbrIel was offering her what she wanted—a shot at Briggs. But the price was steep. She knew she was about to shake hands with the devil, but she would gladly sign that contract if it meant revenge and retribution. Eliminating an NSA team was no small task, and it would put her squarely in the crosshairs of every law enforcement and intelligence agency in the country.

"What else is new?" she whispered under her breath.

She typed back.

"Deal, give me the location."

The response came immediately, providing coordinates and details about a secure NSA facility.

Mags turned to Cole and the rest of her team. "Change of plans, boys. We've got a new target."

Cole raised an eyebrow. "What about Briggs?"

"Briggs will come later," Mags said, her voice stoic and cold.

Chapter 33
NSA Facility
Location Unknown, 2021

The world came groggily back into focus for Violet. What had been nagging pain and a stabbing, throbbing headache had now rolled into waves of tingling pins and needles along her arms and legs. It felt as if every hair follicle on her body was electric. The sweet chemical taste of burnt sugar ran down the back of her throat from the Narcan that had been blasted into her sinuses.

"Damn," she groaned as she sat up slowly.

"Yeah, you went down hard, V." Archie and Grover were leaning over her holding a med kit, each of them looking at her and one another and back again. "You gonna make it?" Archie asked.

"Fuck off," Violet snarled as she grabbed a nearby chair and slid into its cushioned seat.

"Yeah. She's okay." Grover winked at Archie.

"What did I miss?"

Grover and Archie slid back to their respective seats. Archie replied, "Well, you passed the fuck out and we had to save you, so we honestly haven't done much other than watch you sleep and make sure you didn't choke to death on your own barf."

"Super. But what's next? Did y'all have any strokes of genius while I was dying or not?"

Grover chimed in, "So the psych idea is a possibility. Archie and I think that if we can get gAbrIel stuck in a moral or ethical quandary, he might get wrapped in an infinite loop of indecision long enough for us to lock him down."

"Pretend I didn't just have a stroke. Break that down for me. I get the infinite loop part, just like a program that can't stop running and goes nowhere. But explain how we get him there." Violet leaned back and pressed her fingers to the bridge of her nose.

"When we were on that call, he got stuck on that question that was asked about how he could be a god with nobody to be God over. He took a long time to answer. So, he is obviously still learning, and his thought process isn't completely shut off to new ideas or concepts. If we can give him a real humdinger of a question, he might get stuck on it. Then we ping the shit out of him, figure out what server he is currently on and in what data center, and have the Navy or Air Force blow it the hell up. That's as good as I got." Grover shrugged.

"Yeah, that's about the gist of it." Archie sighed.

"What about the 'I am a god, and I am everywhere' thing? If we just get him in one box, isn't he still out there?"

"Maybe," Archie said. "But so far, he has shown up pretty much one off. So best guess is he really sees himself as all-powerful, a god, whatever, and God doesn't make copies of himself. It's a long shot, but it's the only option we have left."

"Good enough for government work. Spin it up." Violet gagged at the taste that gurgled up in the back of her throat and burnt her nostrils. "Fuck the VA."

C:\

REVELATIONS 2:5

2ND MONTH, 5TH DAY...

PENANCE.

Chapter 34

NSA Facility
Location Unknown, 2021

Archie and Grover laid the trap for their final shot at gAbrIel.

Violet pushed her chair into a dark corner of the room for a few minutes of rest and quiet.

Grover pointed at the TV on the ops floor. "Says special alert."

Violet peeked out from under her hand and zeroed in on the screen.

President Cruz was sitting at a desk with an American flag draped on the wall behind her. This was obviously not the West Wing, as the wall was devoid of windows and the background was the dull gray color of government-issued concrete.

"She's in the bunker, dude." Archie stood, crossing his arms. "This can't be good."

Cruz spoke.

"My fellow Americans, I come to you tonight with a heavy heart. We have lost American lives across the world, and our way of life is under threat. While recent online and social media activity indicate that the US is on the brink of war with the nation of China, I assure you that is not the case. Any report or publication you have seen that refers to that current state of geopolitics is simply false. Let me explain to you what is occurring and why I am giving this brief from a secure location…"

The feed suddenly cut off. The screen winked out for a second and came back on. The only picture was the emergency alert system logo and the nagging, buzzing tone with the words "Standby for Further Instructions" scrolling across the black screen.

The EAS system shut off; the screen winked out again. The picture came back, but this time, the chyron where the EAS should have been simply read 2:5. The numbers continuously rolled across the screen, filling it from edge to edge.

"What in the hell is that?" Archie and Grover said simultaneously.

Violet's eyes went wide as she looked across the room at the calendar. "Look at the date, it's February 5th. 2, 5. Today."

"Jesus, gAbrIel said that on the call. But it was a Bible verse or something, right?" Archie whipped his head around at Grover. "We fucking missed it."

Grover pointed at his computer. "Look at the screen. It's a live feed from a traffic cam in DC."

The image was high resolution—the catastrophe was massive. The White House had been smashed to rubble; the only part left standing was the pillars in the front of the structure and parts of the front gate. A smoldering crater sat where the seat of world power once had been.

On the corner of the screen, the feed switched as a motion-detecting camera picked up on activity down Pennsylvania Avenue. A black bolt flashed across the screen before a massive fireball and concussive explosion destroyed the US Treasury building. The camera's zoom was snapping back and forth as it tried to adjust to the plume of smoke and dust that billowed from where the building had been.

"Oh shit!" Archie shouted.

"Yeah, I see it," Violet snapped back.

"No, not that one. Another one."

Archie's finger was pointed at another live feed camera that was across the street from the US Mint on Washington Avenue. Another black streak slung across the screen seconds before the building erupted in a violent clash of stone and mortar rocketing towards the sky. The camera signal went out as a fast-moving cloud of ash and rock filled the screen.

"Jesus. He just took out the whole federal banking system in one shot. The White House, the Treasury, the Mint, and the HQ for the IRS. Gone."

"No faith in the money system or the economy in the most powerful country in the world and the globe's financial powerhouse, and oh, the possible killing of the president. Yeah, shit just got real." Archie fell back in his chair.

Violet lowered her head. "This is it. He told us it was coming."

"What punishment? Apocalypse?" Archie asked incredulously, his voice trailing off.

Violet replied. "Penance."

Part 3 Coming Soon

www.ingramcontent.com/pod-product-compliance
Lightning Source LLC
Chambersburg PA
CBHW061539120525
26539CB00014B/544